What a Christmas Kerfuffle!

A MADISON COUNTY NOVEL

BOOK TWO

Mary Buchanan

Brass Rag Press

ISBN: 978-1-7368109-3-4

DEDICATION

I dedicate this book to my former students from Madison High School, Madison County High School, Hamilton County High School, Paxon School for Advanced Studies, First Coast High School, Frank H. Peterson Academies, A. Philip Randolph Academies, and The Broadway Bunch from Madison Elementary School. You inspired me and gave me immense joy. I treasure every wonderful memory.

ACKNOWLEDGMENTS

Special Thanks to
Cheri Roman, Editor
Lisa Flournoy, Web designer
Tania from Get Covers, Cover design
Esayo Tetteh, Reader
Larry Barefield, Reader
My sisters, Jo Willis and Jackie Gardner (and her husband, Pat), for their continuous encouragement.
Our son, Michael, for cooking meals when I did not want to stop writing!

CONTENTS

Chapter 1

Liz Bradford, Vice President of Bradford Inn Enterprises, chose to stare at the beautiful St. Johns River instead of focusing on the unique driving skills of her Uber driver. She bit a fingernail as Macy weaved between eighteen-wheelers and service trucks as if taxi drivers owned the highway this time of day.

"This traffic is horrendous! Maybe we should slow down a bit."

"Don't worry. I got this," Macy responded.

Liz welcomed the reprieve from the horrific commuter quagmire when her cell phone rang. While Macy listened for radio announcements of wrecks on I-95, Liz gripped her hand on the center armrest and listened to her brother, Bryan, a chef on a sabbatical in Paris.

Liz glanced toward the bridge ahcad. "Oops!"

"What's wrong, baby sister?"

"It's rush hour!"

The driver had experience at maneuvering on the busy expressway at this hour. However, crossing the Dames Point Bridge was risky because high school students and teachers from three local schools headed home or to part-time jobs at 2:45 p.m. Other industrial factories released their employees thirty minutes later. Transport truck drivers from Jax Port claimed highway ownership in the afternoon too.

Today was a typical sunny winter day on the major highway racetrack to the Jacksonville train depot. Mesmerized, Liz gazed as

Macy checked her side mirror and steered the car behind a long black hearse. Liz covered her eyes with her hands, anticipating a rear-end collision.

Due to an appointment with a client, Liz was late for the train to Vermont. Dressed in a pin-striped business suit, she fidgeted in the back seat, talking to her brother on her cell phone, pretending to be unaware of the rush-hour congestion.

When the car slowed to a creep, Liz glanced at the crowded lanes and stared at the top of the beautiful bridge ahead. "Hm, Bryan?"

"Yes."

"I think I have to end this call."

"Why?"

"I'm going to have a nervous breakdown." Liz looked at the other cars forming a parking lot. "Macy, why has traffic slowed to a snail's pace?"

Liz glanced around the expressway and saw cars stalled in three lanes. "What's happening?"

"The radio reported an accident on the other side of the bridge," said Macy, "Don't worry. I'll get you to that depot with time to spare."

"How? Not one car is moving forward. My train leaves at 4:00 p.m.!"

"Trust me. The police will clear the highway in a few minutes."

Liz scanned the extensive line of vehicles waiting behind Macy's Ford Edge. The man in the dark blue Porsche on Liz's left made phone calls during the delay. On the right, a young female driving a white Rubicon with a surfboard attached to the roof danced to her loud music. Liz was the only person demonstrating any stress, twiddling her thumbs as the car idled in the middle lane.

"How many minutes to the terminal from here?" asked Liz as she rearranged her shopping bags on the black leather car seat.

"It's not far. You won't miss the train today," Macy glanced in the rearview mirror.

"Oh, my!" Liz pounded her forehead with her right hand.

"Liz?" asked Bryan over the phone.

"Oh, there's been an accident."

"Are you okay?"

"Not me! It's on the other side of the bridge."

"Oh, okay. Relax. The driver will get you to your destination."

"I hope so." Liz looked at her cabbie, "Macy?"

"Yes."

"My brother says you will get me to the train on time."

"Smart brother," responded the driver, checking her watch.

"Bryan, did you hear Macy's comment?" asked Liz.

"No, what did she say?"

"Macy said my brother should come home for Christmas."

Bryan paused, "I'm not sure I could even get a plane ticket at this point."

"Please try."

"Okay, but I can't make any promises. Love you. Don't miss your train."

"I won't."

"Liz, are you on speaker?"

"No."

"Then, how does Macy know I am in Paris and not coming home for Christmas?"

"My Uber driver has ESP."

"Sure, she does."

"Please think about coming home. Don't you miss us?"

"Of course," Bryan conceded, "Okay, I'll check on it."

"Great! Thanks for calling. It was perfect timing."

"Are you calm now?"

"Let's say I am cautiously optimistic."

"Think positive. You always do. Love you, bye."

Liz reclined on the seat and closed her eyes, drumming on the armrest with her fingers. She would use this time wisely. She mentally checked her Christmas list and remembered she must buy a present for Sam, the bartender and her best friend at The Bradford Inn. She grabbed her phone and found a Green Bay Packers jersey for sale online with guaranteed delivery by Christmas Eve. *Sam loves that team! He will never expect that gift from me.*

Next, she focused on her first recruiting job for The Bradford Inn. Although Liz was the daughter of the president and owner of the inn, she took her job seriously and worked hard. She created promotional packages for associations for annual officer meetings and business training.

Since many charitable organizations chose Jacksonville for their home offices, Liz kicked off her initiative this week in Jaguar country. It was an intelligent decision.

Macy announced, "The problem must have cleared. Cars are cresting the hill from the other side."

"Great! We have forty minutes." Liz tapped her right foot.

The automobiles proceeded slowly. By the time the vehicle reached the top of the bridge, traffic was rolling as expected. The exit sign for the terminal stood in the distance.

With twenty-five minutes left, the Vermont native arrived at the front door of Amtrack. Having traveled to the southern city by train on Monday, Liz was familiar with the building. Saying a quick goodbye to Macy, Liz walked briskly toward the main entrance, not anticipating long lines of passengers inside.

When the electric doors opened, she realized having an appointment after lunch on the day of her departure was a big mistake, especially during a holiday week. Christmas travelers scurried toward the check-in line. Long rows formed as people prepared for baggage check. She panicked as holiday commuters with children and packages rushed by her.

As she maneuvered through the noisy crowd, she barely heard the phone ring when her mother called. Liz stopped abruptly in the middle of passenger traffic and searched for her phone hidden in her purse.

Her sudden stop caused a traffic jam, and one gentleman's body slammed into Liz. A chain reaction followed. Her luggage rolled away, and her phone and packages crashed to the floor in the opposite direction. Everyone near the area heard the noise and looked at the chaos caused by the beautiful woman near the entrance.

Embarrassed, Liz apologized to the gentleman and the group standing behind her and quickly retrieved her phone.

"Mom, there was an accident on the freeway, but finally, I made it to the depot." Gathering packages and luggage, Liz listened as her mother delivered disturbing news.

"The Grady Group canceled their gig?" asked Liz as she hurried forward.

"Yes, a few minutes ago."

"They are under contract!" Liz pressed the cell phone closer to her ear.

"Well, they are not coming."

"When I get on the train, I'll get right on it."

"Sweetheart, it's okay. I took care of it," answered Annabelle Bradford, the president and one-third owner of the family business.

What has my dear boss done this time? "Mother, I'll call you in a few minutes. Don't worry about the entertainment for the hotel," said Liz, "I'll fix the problem."

After Liz secured her phone in her left hand, she navigated through the congestion. She heard the departure announcement for her train and questioned why she had not changed her navy spiked heels to running shoes. *What else can happen to ruin my day?*

A Christmas medley by the familiar, sad, scratchy voice of Jake Jones, the famous country music star, followed the intercom message. Liz did not have fond memories of that man, her high school sweetheart. *What nut listens to Jake Jones during any season? I should have checked my horoscope for today.*

Liz gasped, "Maybe I shouldn't get on the train!"

Liz realized her packages were slipping. She abruptly stopped to adjust them. Unfortunately, her hasty actions caused another calamity. People dodged her boxes as several holiday gifts slid across a renovated section of the tiled floor. Liz gritted her teeth and clenched her hands in frustration.

Yards away from Liz, a young male traveler wearing a royal blue shirt with a large-mouth bass on the back and a smaller fish embroidered over the front pocket stood patiently in the security checkpoint line. Another loud crash drew his attention toward the entrance to the building. He focused on the auburn-haired young lady, who stared as her packages scattered in several directions.

The gentleman couldn't leave to help her because an officer was checking his suitcase. He watched as the well-dressed woman stretched her neck and rolled her head. *Security should personally escort that human disaster for damage control. Hopefully, she is traveling south.*

After gathering her bags again, Liz rushed toward the check-in desk. In haste, she walked too close to an oversized Christmas elf, knocking down the heavy, life-size plastic ornament.

Although Liz felt the stares of the other passengers, she refused to acknowledge them. She figured people were running to get away from her by now. She must remove that country singer's music and bad memories from her thoughts. She inhaled slowly and exhaled.

After a thoughtful lady assisted Liz in gathering her bags and placing the Christmas elf upright, Liz paused again. She took a moment to carefully separate her purchases, arranging them equally to carry in each hand. Her frustration was all Jake Jones' fault! She walked fast but focused long enough to observe her surroundings to avoid another collision.

After checking her departure time, she fumbled for her numerous Christmas purchases and briefcase and ran to the shortest security line. *Jake, please finish singing that song! Somebody, destroy that awful CD*! *Listeners want to hear real Christmas music!*

With all requirements completed, Liz approached the train carefully. When she presented her ticket, the packages in that hand slipped, and her briefcase clattered along the scuffed concrete.

By this time, Liz was tired of being the center of attention for the holiday travelers. She did not notice the gentleman as he approached the disaster queen. Liz accepted her briefcase without looking in his direction.

Grateful, Liz said, "Thanks."

However, when she glanced to see who had assisted her, her knight in shining armor had disappeared. She adjusted her packages and managed to board without losing anything else. The stressed female traveler briefly leaned against the wall, paused, and breathed, relieved to be on the locomotive. She almost destroyed the depot, but she made it.

As she maneuvered through the train's corridor, looking for compartment thirty-six, Liz warmly greeted other travelers. She noticed the door was slightly open when she passed the sleeping cabin closest to hers. Liz overheard a man's deep sexy voice. She stopped when the words "The Bradford Inn" were spoken.

CABIN 37

"And who picked The Bradford Inn as our destination anyway? There's another hotel in that town," Deep Voice vented.

A sweet, firm female voice responded, "Dear, I remember what happened there."

"Mother, we always stay home for Christmas. I don't understand why we leave Florida's sunshine for cold Vermont. Have you considered that you and Marty may get pneumonia?"

"Sweetheart, I understand your concerns. However, your father needs to escape from the bank and leave Orlando. He won't be able to drive to the office from the inn in Wellington. The weatherman said the town may have eighteen inches of snow on Christmas Day. I hope you packed warm clothes."

"I did. At least Wellington is a small town."

"That's the right attitude, Son," encouraged Jill Harvelle.

"And there are great college games scheduled."

"Yes. And you, Dad, and Charlie will have an exciting time watching football."

Max realized the train was in motion. "I can't change my mind now."

"Trust me. Marty and I walked through the hotel, and it was grand. You will be surprised at how different the place looks. The new owners renovated the entire facility. Don't focus on old memories. I know what is best for you. I promise it's going to be wonderful!"

A client's call interrupted Max's conference with his mother.

"I must take this call. Talk to you later. Love you." Max switched to the guy on the other line. "Hey, Jerrod. Any other issues?"

"No, you solved the problem. We have an important client on a Zoom conference call tomorrow, the last business meeting before the holiday break. My boss would have my hide if you hadn't found the problem and repaired the computer program. Thanks."

"Glad to hear everything is working properly."

"Email the bill, and we will get you paid before Christmas. Are you taking a week off, as usual?"

"Yeah, I am on the train to Wellington, Vermont, now."

"I thought your family got together in Orlando every year."

"According to Mother, Dad needs a change of scenery."

"Hey, I have a friend who lives in Surrey. It's about thirty miles from Wellington. Her family practically owns the town. Why don't I call her and see if she is available for dinner one evening?"

"Thanks for the kind gesture, but you know I avoid women. Anyway, I don't have time to do a background check on your recommendation."

"Very funny. This girl is a great catch."

"I'm sure she is, but my mother has scheduled every moment. She is planning something special for the family this year."

"What?"

"Only Santa Claus knows!"

Chapter 2

CABIN 36

After Liz entered her room, she temporarily forgot her mother's emergency call. She dropped her packages on the floor and leaned against the door. The weary traveler felt as if she had passed through a hazing incident in a sorority. She figured security was relieved she was on the train. Someone over the public speaker probably announced, "The destructive cyclone has left the building."

Liz walked to the window and wondered about the conversation she had just heard. What horrible situation occurred at The Bradford Inn five years ago? It must have been terrible because Deep Voice hated returning there.

As she contemplated the situation, she reorganized her suitcase, a habit she followed when traveling for the family company. Then, she carefully stacked all her packages in the small closet. After glancing around the room for stray articles, she opened her computer and reviewed her reports on the latest Jacksonville contracts. She checked her goal sheet.

She had met with ten organizations on this business trip and had signed with five. Three groups had liked her proposal but must wait until January at their annual board meetings to make the final decisions. Two prospects had rejected her proposal, claiming their families preferred the beach for business trips. However, several officers of the companies had requested information about personal family vacations.

She wrote herself a memo to leave vacation brochures at offices in the future, and she added her idea about appointment timing in Jacksonville to her procedures file. She exhaled slowly.

She stopped for a moment and gazed out the window at the farmland scenes as the sound of the wheels gliding down the tracks soothed her. The family hadn't been informed of any significant incident at the hotel when it had purchased the property from Uncle James Bradford three years ago.

As she contemplated that situation, Liz reflected on the irony of her view from the train. The River City served as a major shipping port for the east coast. Yet, within the Jacksonville city limits lay patches of farmland spotted with cows and goats or timberlands, tall and majestic, standing along a slow, running river.

The view reminded her of life, simple but complicated. The scene was peaceful. Looking at the beautiful landscape, it didn't take long for her heartbeat to slow down and the tension in her shoulders to ease. She thought of the guy next door and hoped he had a better experience at her family inn this holiday.

The song, 'Taking Care of Business,' blared from her phone. *Oh, I forgot to call Mom!*

"Hey," Liz spoke in an apologetic tone.

"Did you make it in time, Sweetheart?"

"Yes, I just got settled. I'm sorry I didn't call back. Okay, what happened to our singing quartet?"

"All of them are down with the flu." Annabelle didn't sound disappointed.

"That's not good," Liz exhaled, "Don't worry. I'll check my entertainment contact list." Liz grabbed her notebook and pen. "It will be tough finding a replacement this late in the season; however, somebody will be available."

"First, tell me about the new contracts." Annabelle avoided further conversation about the entertainment for the lounge.

"We have five association conferences scheduled for May through June. One is booking a week for its annual board meeting in January in two years. I'm finishing the reports now. How about I email them to you when I finish?"

"Wow, your recruitment idea was a good one. Proud of you, dear." Annabelle was anxious to get off the phone. "Enough about business. We'll talk tomorrow. Enjoy your ride home, Sweetheart."

"I will. Don't hang up. We need to talk about the entertainment for the inn," Liz reminded Annabelle.

"Uh, Liz, I already found a solution to that problem."

Liz closed her computer, "Mrs. Annabelle, what did you do without consulting me?"

Annabelle responded quickly, "You won't believe it. I got lucky and found someone to fill in for the whole week."

Sensing something familiar in her mother's attitude, Liz asked, "Who?"

"Don't worry; a CMA winner is good, and he will draw a crowd."

Liz rephrased her question. "Who is 'he'?"

"Now, this was an emergency. The inn is booked solid. Our guests expect quality entertainment. He was available, so I hired him."

Liz chose another avenue since the boss skillfully dodged her daughter's questions. "Mother, is Jake Jones the 'he' you are talking about?"

Annabelle stalled for a minute, thinking of the best way to frame her answer, "He has written several new songs and wants to debut them at our inn."

"I wish you would have addressed that issue with me before you finalized it."

"If you think about it, having a CMA award and Grammy winner perform here is great publicity."

"You know how I feel about that man!" Liz exhaled, "I would prefer that we contract with someone else. I'll find a group more appropriate for our clientele."

"Sometimes people change, and doors magically open. You know, we see love bloom here, especially at Christmas."

"We are not writing a TV commercial," Liz sighed, "Please tell me Jake has not signed the contract yet."

Annabelle hesitated before she answered, "He signed."

Liz drummed her fingers on her computer. "Of course, he did. Well -." Her shoulders tensed.

"Sweetheart? Jake has one request."

"What?" Liz exhaled.

"He wants to talk to you before his first performance. I think you should listen to him."

"Mrs. Annabelle?"

"Yes."

"My feelings for that man have not magically changed."

"I know, but this may be the perfect time to listen to him. You have not spoken to him since high school graduation. Liz, maybe your old sweetheart needs to clear his conscience."

"Well, he almost caused me to lose my college scholarship. Do you remember?"

"Of course I do."

Liz paused, "Okay, please tell your hired performer I got his message. Also, instruct the superstar to tell Sam when he will be rehearsing at our facility. You didn't give him a suite as part of his contract, did you?"

Annabelle remained quiet.

"Oh, Mother!"

"Well, to be honest. I gave Jake the same contract you gave to the Grady Group."

"Mother?"

"Yes?"

"In the future, please inform me before making major decisions regarding entertainment. That is one of the responsibilities you hired me to do."

"Yes, I will, but I feel good about this option," Annabelle sighed, "Liz, something tells me this holiday will be spectacular for you."

"Okay. I'll email my notes regarding the new contracts in a few minutes. Call if you have any questions."

"And don't worry about Jake. He's different. You'll see."

"I won't. Love you."

"Dear?"

"Yes."

"Did I mention Sam's daughter is expecting her second child?"

"No," Liz took a deep breath.

"That's two grandchildren for him."

"Thanks for sharing that information." Liz looked at the ceiling and rolled her eyes. "I'm happy for Sam. See you tomorrow."

"Your poor father didn't get to meet his grandchildren before he died," Annabelle added, "Isn't that sad?"

Liz paused and bit her lower lip. "Maybe Bryan will meet a beautiful woman in Paris and fall madly in love."

Annabelle sat straight in her chair, "Do you think he has met someone special?"

"Uh, he may have by now."

"I think I will call my favorite son and see how he is doing. Love you."

"Good idea."

Liz shook her head. Her mother always mentioned the grandchild thing when Liz was away from home. She thought her mother believed the idea remained in Liz's mind longer. The tired daughter stretched her neck, moved her head in a circle, and rolled her shoulders. At least her mother was focused on Bryan now. *I'm sorry, Brother. No, not really!*

Liz adjusted her paperwork, but the news of Jake Jones coming home again and entertaining at the inn made it difficult for her to concentrate on business. She didn't want to deal with him. Why wouldn't Jake leave her alone? Did he want to rub his success in her face?

Liz was distracted by loud music coming from the cabin next door. Immediately, she recognized the song from Jake's first album.

She mumbled, "I am not about to listen to that music all night. What have I done to deserve this punishment? I don't remember ever hearing music from another room on this train. Maybe Deep Voice is hard of hearing. He certainly doesn't recognize quality music." *And now I am talking to myself!*

She re-examined the contracts and wrote notes to her mother. She stopped working when the loud music again interrupted her thoughts. Liz remembered that song. It was Jake's most popular and on the charts for weeks. *What am I thinking?*

Liz forced herself to focus and check her spelling and grammar. Jake's songs were always sad. Was he trying to brainwash women? Liz sighed. Her notebook slid off the seat; papers flew everywhere.

Finding it difficult to concentrate, she set her computer aside, grabbed the papers cluttered on the floor, and paced in the small cabin for a minute. Wanting to complete her tasks, Liz ignored the familiar tunes coming from next door and returned to her computer.

Using her editor application, she reviewed the language in her paragraphs. She wondered if success had changed Jake. He was probably more arrogant than in high school. Liz hit the "SEND" key. The sound of that scratchy voice seemed to get a little louder. She turned off the computer and returned to the window seat. She located a business sales manual tucked in her travel bag and read a chapter.

Liz heard Jake crooning thirty minutes later, and the volume had increased again. Deep Voice must be in great pain to listen to that awful sound for that long. *Maybe he lost his hearing at The Bradford Inn. That may be the reason he doesn't want to return.*

Slowly, the movement of the train lulled Liz to sleep.

CABIN 37

While listening to his favorite singer, Max Harvelle contemplated the family conversation on Thanksgiving Day. When Mom declared the family was going to the Green Mountain State for Christmas, Dad asked strange questions. Now that Max had reflected on the situation, he recalled that his father was also surprised by Mom's suggestion.

Marty's husband, Charlie, looked shocked at the idea and stared at his wife. However, Mom insisted on the destination, never wavering. Of course, Marty supported Mom's crazy decision.

Max offered his home as an alternate holiday venue, but his mother was adamant about returning to Vermont. He could solve complex math problems and fix a major computer issue, but he didn't know why his family traveled 1,356 miles to snow-covered mountains for Christmas. A man couldn't even play golf in Vermont in December.

He chuckled because Mom and Marty preferred a hot climate. Maybe someone sent Mom a romantic, cozy Christmas card last year, inspiring this crazy plan. Had she forgotten how cold the weather was in the north this time of year? This trip may prove to be the funniest adventure in Max's life.

He turned up the volume. After the divorce, he found solace in the famous singer's mellow tunes. His family often ridiculed him because Max listened so much to the quirky, good old country boy.

But Max was an "old soul" even though he was a "techie." He relaxed next to the large window and turned up the volume a little more. He observed the view outside as the train traveled parallel to a slow-flowing river.

He saw an older man dressed in camouflage, fishing from the sandy bank. The fisherman sat in a flimsy lawn chair positioned near a roaring fire. The calming scene reminded Max of sitting in a camping chair, casting his reel off his wooden dock at Cherry Lake, a rural Madison County community.

When Max was sixteen, he and a group of friends had traveled through the tiny town during springtime and had seen the beautiful wildflowers blooming along the roadside. As he navigated the countryside, he had felt as though he belonged there. Max remembered the peaceful, scenic region in North Florida throughout high school and college. He told his friends he hoped to live there one day.

In his last year of college, Max fell in love with the perfect woman who wanted an expensive wedding at The Bradford Inn in Wellington. He tried to make her happy, but when he followed his dream to live in the land of wildflowers, his bride never adjusted to that calm lifestyle. She preferred hectic city life.

Max realized too late how different he and Becca were. He waited for her to understand life in a serene, small community was not exciting all the time. The Cherry Lake area provided a wonderful place to rear children, interact with neighbors, and live a peaceful life.

His wife had asked for a divorce after one year. Becca preferred the hustle and bustle of the big, busy city. When friends heard about the divorce, they acknowledged that Max and Becca were total opposites and were not surprised at her decision to leave. The last time he had heard, she was searching for a rich husband in Atlanta.

Max was happy as a single man. However, his mom, Jill, whom he loved dearly, didn't believe her boy could be content living alone with a computer as his sidekick. The good son avoided Mother's earnest attempts to help him find a new soul mate. He constantly received cards with cute photos of his friends and their families, providing precious grandchildren for their mothers.

Weekly, he talked with beautiful women whom his mother had persuaded to call him. To his mother's disappointment, Max never offered an invitation to any of them.

Max thought about the week ahead as he watched the farm scenes roll by his train window. This holiday season was different. For the first time, he would return to the venue where he married Becca. His cell phone rang.

"Hello."

"Hey, Max, am I calling at a bad time?"

"Sydnee, perfect timing."

"JJ and I want you to have Christmas lunch with us if you are going to be in Madison."

"Thanks for the invitation, but I am joining the family in Vermont."

"You couldn't talk them out of that trip?"

"No, and believe me, I tried," Max sighed.

"Well, accidentally miss the train," suggested his friend.

"Too late. I'm on it now."

"Heck, I should have called you last night."

"I think my mother would leave me out of the will if I told her I had chosen the Wildflowers over her."

Sydnee laughed. "You're probably right. Listen, have a great Christmas. Call Diane if you need money, Margo if you need a date, and me if you need advice. We're available twenty-four hours a day."

"I will not forget that."

"By the way, save the February 14th date. JJ and I are getting married that day. An invitation is in the mail. You can bring a guest. Margo said she would get you a plus one if you need it. She promises a beautiful lady."

"I'll put it on my calendar and tell Margo I will call her about that date."

"Great. Enjoy your holiday."

"You, too. Merry Christmas! Bye."

Sydnee Watson, Margo Cashwell, and Diane Harris were the first people he had met when he had moved to Madison County. Margo was Max's realtor. Dianne was one of the civic enthusiasts, and Sydnee ran The Wildflowers B & B. As teenagers, the ladies had earned the reputation of the Wildflowers due to their tendency to break the rules.

Max was thankful for their friendship. If he could meet a woman like one of them, he would consider marriage again. Hmm, on second thought, forget that idea. He didn't think there was another one around.

Max looked at his watch and thought about dinner. He listened to the rest of Jake's song. In Max's opinion, his favorite singer was good for the soul.

If I have learned anything in the last five years, it's that my life is better without a woman!

Chapter 3

When Liz awakened, she could not believe Jake Jones was still crooning next door. *What is wrong with that guy?* The poor soul must own every one of the vocalist's songs. Finally, she couldn't listen to that noise anymore. She chose to leave the room and go to the dining car.

The music next door magically stopped when her hand touched the doorknob to exit her cabin. Liz jerked her hand back. *My first Christmas miracle! No more Jake Jones!* She grabbed her notebook, pen, and purse and stepped outside her door.

When she heard another door shut, she glanced to her left. The super music fan was locking his door. When the man with dark brown hair, a perfectly shaved beard, and a pair of gorgeous green eyes returned her stare, Liz attempted to secure her door, but she couldn't get the card in the lock. *Oh, no, why won't this thing work?* In the process, she dropped her notebook, and her pen rolled between Deep Voice's shoes.

"Do you need any assistance with your lock?" Max stooped to pick up Liz's notebook and pen. He recognized the lady as Whack-a-do Wanda, who had nocked out the Christmas elf at the depot. He tried not to smile.

"No, I have it. Thanks." *Please fit in the lock. Heck, what am I doing wrong?*

After a second attempt, the door card fit. *How embarrassing!* Liz accepted her notebook and pen. *The man may not have a brain, but he is a hunk. What a cute smile, or is he laughing at me?*

Max motioned for her to proceed forward, and he followed, noticing her incredible figure. As they met other guests in the corridor, Max observed Emerald Eyes always speaking first to everyone. *She must be in sales. Yeah, that's it. How can she be successful? She's a klutz!*

Liz concluded Deep Voice must be in a state of depression after listening to off-key country music for hours. *If he is communicating with anyone he meets, it must be nonverbal. Hearing the sad songs of the CMA winner has diminished the man's capacity to speak to people, or he could be a snob.*

When Liz arrived at the dining car, the area was packed with guests. She knew Deep Voice was behind her. She smelled his fantastic cologne. Of course, there was only one table left. Lady luck was failing her again tonight. First, Jake's music, and now, a small place for two. She was hungry. She assumed the good-looking snob behind her was too. Liz looked at Deep Voice over her shoulder.

She asked, "Would you like to share this table?"

"Sure," he responded. He wondered if the pretty lady would work or knock over the table during her meal.

The dining car windows, decorated in red and green ribbon, coordinated well with the holiday carnations in short vases placed on each counter. Accessories with a Christmas theme accented the entrance. Soft caroling music played to entertain the patrons.

When the new stranger pulled out a chair for her, Liz concluded that her handsome cabin neighbor had excellent manners. Because of the closeness of the small dining situation, when Liz sat down and placed her notebook on the bright tablecloth, she immediately knocked her knife and spoon onto the floor.

A server, who moved quickly to replace the flatware, handed menus to the couple and requested drink orders.

Max avoided eye contact because he knew he would laugh. He expected Emerald Eyes to fall out of her chair next. He watched the pretty woman out of the corner of his eyes, waiting for her next act of destruction.

Liz turned her attention to the menu. She checked to see if the battery-operated candle flame was secure, fearful she would break the center if she accidentally knocked over the lighted decoration. *I think he is laughing at me!*

When the server placed the water glasses for each guest, neither traveler could avoid the new person across the table.

Now, Liz would think of Jake whenever she looked at this guy. She erased that country-western out-of-tune singer from her mind. Without thinking, Liz stretched her neck and rolled her head.

Ugh, there goes her head ritual. Whack-a-do Wanda may be going to attack the table next. As a precaution, he opted to hold his water glass. Max turned his head so the lady couldn't see his smile.

Liz stared at the menu even though she knew what she planned to order. *It is possible the man across the table may have a learning disability. That's it! And he's hard of hearing, too. Everything makes sense now, but he is cute.*

*M*ax checked out the dinner options. *Maybe I'm wrong. She may be a schoolteacher who has lost her mind.* Max studied Emerald Eyes as she glanced at her menu. First, she frowned as if she hated the food list. Then, he observed her facial features soften. *Wow! Now, she is pretty, with her sexy hair curling over her shoulders. Obviously, she loves something on the food list.* He hoped she wasn't one of those diet women who ate crumbs.

Sensing someone was watching her, Liz raised her eyes and slowly lowered her menu to find the man with the deep voice staring at her intently. They gazed at each other momentarily, wondering who would break first. A server arrived with coffee. Max and Liz mentally forgot the staring competition.

Max loved Emerald Eyes' competitive spirit. He couldn't resist. "Did you have a difficult day?"

"When you say difficult, what are you referencing?"

"I saw you attack the Christmas elf back at the station."

Liz slowly smiled until she grinned, "You saw that?"

"Yeah, I would have rushed to save the big holiday ornament, but I was engaged in a security check at the time of the elf's demise."

"For your information, Santa's helper did not sustain any mortal wounds."

"Looked to me like you whacked him pretty good."

Liz giggled, "Don't worry. He has sisters who will deliver your present on Christmas Eve."

"I appreciate that from the depths of my heart." Max looked around the dining car. "Looks as if everyone got hungry at the same time tonight."

"I know I am," responded Liz.

Liz noticed the man across from her was not wearing a wedding ring. Then she remembered the phone call she had overheard. *He's probably divorced. So, he is hard to live with, is partially deaf, and lacks musical sense.* She concluded the only thing going for this guy was his voice and his looks.

When Liz traveled, she never used her real name when dealing with strangers. She used the alias "Sarah" when riding the train. It was a fun game for her to play during an often-dull trip. She would remember where they met if she ran into the same guy later. It was a safety strategy for a woman traveling alone. If Deep Voice was a fan of Jake's, he might be the mysterious stranger from the twilight zone. Being an admirer of Jake Jones was a clear signal something was wrong with the man across the table.

"I'm Sarah."

"Max."

Liz asked, "Do you travel by train often?"

Max sighed, "Some."

Liz said, "Me, too. I prefer land over sky."

"So do I." Max examined the food list. "The menu appears to offer several good choices."

"Everything on the menu is good, but the spaghetti." Liz looked at Deep Voice, wondering if he would challenge her opinion.

Max continued to study his choices, "What's wrong with the spaghetti?"

"The chef doesn't have my recipe."

He glanced at Liz, "Are you a culinarian?"

"No."

"You don't look Italian. Is it a family recipe?"

"No."

When the server returned for their food orders, Liz said, "I'll have chicken salad on chopped, crispy lettuce, with a dill pickle on the side."

"I'll have the same but add buttery crackers."

"Good choice," said Liz.

"So, are we playing twenty questions, or will you tell me about the spaghetti?" asked Max.

Liz liked his assertiveness. *He can think a little. Jake Jones has not done permanent mental damage.* "I make a mean spaghetti sauce which my family loves. I ordered it for dinner on the first business trip on this train. I think it came right out of a can. No seasonings. No flavor."

"Thanks for the warning."

Max watched the city as the locomotive cruised along the tracks. He admired the colorful Christmas lights, remembering when he had ridden home from Wellington, Vermont, five years ago.

"This is a beautiful sight with all the holiday lights on display," said Max.

Liz checked the clock on her cell phone and leaned over toward Max, "I don't want to scare you, but it may get eerie for the next sixty seconds."

"Why?"

Soon, the train entered a tunnel, and the train lights blinked. Then, the dining car was in total darkness for less than a minute. Liz used her cell phone light to brighten her face.

Liz spoke quietly to avoid scaring the other guests, "If there is a terrorist attack using this tunnel, these are the people you will go with into eternity." She looked around at the guests. "Doesn't that scare you?"

Max looked at Sarah, trying to decide if she was serious. He looked around at the people in the dining car, noticing everyone was silent. Several people used their cell phones for lights. Neither he nor Sarah spoke until the train was out of the tunnel.

"There is good news. No terrorist attack tonight, and you won't die from the chef's spaghetti, either." Liz winked at him.

Max relaxed. He acknowledged Scary Sarah was beautiful and had a sense of humor. Of course, she could be a lunatic if she taught school, but the lady looked too young. Maybe she taught elementary students. No, the woman had too much hair on her head. He was glad there had been only one table left tonight.

As they enjoyed their meal, Liz listened as Max talked endlessly about how he was a huge fan of Jake Jones. Max knew everything about her former classmate, including that the famous singer grew up in Vermont.

"I'm a rock 'n' roll girl, myself." *Can this man talk about something else?*

Max teased, "Never grew up, huh?"

Liz looked straight at Max and confessed, "Some might say that."

After dinner, they ordered wine. Max shared family stories of Christmas, his work, and aerophobia.

"What happened to cause your fear of flying?" asked Liz.

"On a return flight from a business trip to New York, the airplane filled with smoke. I thought I was going to die. I called my dad, and he talked to me throughout the incident. The plane made an emergency landing in North Carolina. I rented a car and drove to Madison County. I vowed never to get on a plane again."

"I understand that anxiety. When I was a college freshman, my parents encouraged me to take a course that included a field trip to regions in Europe. I spent the summer flying from one country to another. I had a tremendous educational experience until one flight."

"Did you have an emergency landing?"

"No, our plane hit severe air pockets on a flight out of France. It was terrifying. The following week, a plane similar to the one our tour group chartered crashed somewhere in Europe. I prayed and asked the Lord to get me home. And He did. Nothing or no one will be significant enough to get me on a plane again. No exception to that rule."

Max said, "I've had to fly a couple of times due to time constraints for business, but every flight was stressful. I also avoid that mode of travel most of the time."

"Is this a business trip?" asked Liz.

"No, my family is meeting in Wellington, Vermont, for the holidays."

"That town is beautiful and filled with many family traditions. It's a perfect venue for Christmas, business conventions, and weddings."

"I know. I married at the 'awful' Bradford Inn five years ago during Christmas. My mother insisted my family return this year."

"That's crazy!" Liz exclaimed before thinking about how it might sound.

Max was glad someone agreed with him. "Thanks for seeing it from my point of view. My family usually celebrates holidays in Orlando, where I have lived most of my life."

"So, why the change this year?"

"I don't know. I've tried to figure it out. My former wife, Becca, discovered The Bradford Inn on a website listing grand wedding venues and fell in love with the place. A year later, her dream wedding was everything she wanted. After our first anniversary, she announced she was bored with the simple life and asked for a divorce."

And that's why you listen to all those sad songs by Jake Jones. Liz attempted to sway his opinion on the inn, thinking he would anticipate a happier experience this time.

"I'm sorry about that," said Liz.

"Becca wasn't that difficult to get over."

"Um," Liz didn't know how to react.

"The inn wasn't the problem," said Max.

"But The Bradford Inn triggers bad memories?"

"Yeah. The place reminds me of the biggest mistake of my life."

"The inn is under new management. That information should make your visit more positive this year."

Max asked, "How do you know so much about the place?"

Liz realized she may have given away too much information and reeled off, "That's my destination, also."

Why did that last statement make Max happy? He paused and reminded himself not to be fooled by the beautiful, green-eyed woman sitting across the table. *Don't forget my mantra, man!*

They both sat quietly for a minute. Max wondered why he shared so much personal information with a total stranger. Liz was afraid she had talked too much about her place of employment.

"I propose a toast," said Max.

"Okay."

"May this Christmas erase old memories."

Liz firmly agreed with that salute. It was a challenge to forget Jake Jones since he would be providing the entertainment for the inn this holiday season. What a bummer! She should tell Max that his favorite singer was the featured attraction. That would lift his sad spirits. Oops, she couldn't. How would a person named Sarah know that?

"Sarah, what do you do for a living? Demolition work?"

"I know I gave the impression I'm a klutz several times today, but I am a detailed, organized woman. I arrange conference and business trips for large associations and corporations."

"Do you have a large clientele base?"

"Not at this time." Liz added, "I work in large cities with home offices for various corporations. I like associations because most of them focus on a worthy cause."

"I thought for a minute you might be a schoolteacher."

"Ha, I don't fit that mold." Then, Liz asked, "So, what do you do besides attempt to be a comedian?"

"I own a computer consulting firm. I work from my home office, but sometimes I must travel."

"Do you live in Jacksonville?"

"No, I moved to a small community about a hundred miles west. It's a quaint little place known for its wildflowers blooming everywhere in the spring and summer."

"That sounds like a beautiful place to live and work."

"It is for most people. But my ex hated it."

"I'm not taking up for her, but some people are better suited to city life."

"Yeah, I found that out."

Max found himself comfortable talking with Sarah. "The main problem I cannot get over is Becca's ability to lie. She should have told me the truth about living in the country. I realized too late how different we were." He leaned back in his chair. "I can't believe I shared those feelings with you. I haven't spoken those words to anyone. You're easy to talk to."

"Thanks. Now, I understand why you are anxious about returning to Wellington." *Finally, I meet a nice guy and break his number one rule within five minutes. Girl, you know how to make a great first impression.* Liz hated lying, too.

After talking for hours, another young couple in the dining car joined them in conversation. When Max introduced her as Sarah, Liz's lie was like Pinocchio's nose; her lie grew bigger. She wondered how Max was at forgiving people for stupid safety habits. She couldn't tell him 'Sarah' was not her real name. He wouldn't trust her. *Good grief, I find a man Mother would approve of, and I introduce myself with an alias. If I tell him my name is Liz, he will understand that, won't he? No, Max may think my habit is a sign of a crazy person.* Her intuition convinced her to wait and confess to Deep Voice later.

They shared experiences with the newly married couple until the early morning hours. Back in the cabin, Liz could not go to sleep. For the first time in years, she had enjoyed her evening. She found herself attracted to Max. The only negative Liz could find about the guy was his admiration for a certain country music singer.

When Liz closed her eyes, she thought about the man in the cabin next door. Deep Voice lived in Florida, and she lived in Vermont. However, Florida had many associations based there. The Sunshine State looked better by the hour. What would Max think when Liz admitted she had used an alias? She punched per pillow.

Max had trouble falling asleep, too. *Sarah appears to be interested in what I have to say.* He recalled she never picked up her pen to work. Max propped his pillows against the headboard. *She is nothing like Becca. I'll find her in the morning and ask for her phone number.* Yep, the cold snow in Vermont looked warmer now. Maybe it was time Max stopped avoiding women, especially one with emerald eyes. *At least she is a cute klutz!*

Chapter 4

The following day when the train pulled into Wellington, Liz darted off the train, hoping to get to her car and the inn before the tourist crowd. As she drove out of the terminal, she saw Max standing by the side of the road waiting for The Bradford Inn transit bus.

"You want a ride? I'm going to the inn."

"Yeah. I looked for you this morning."

"Sorry. I leave my car at the station when I take the train."

"Well, I'm glad you saw me. I wanted to tell you how much I enjoyed our dinner last night."

"I did too."

"I appreciate the ride."

"I hope you and your family have a great holiday."

"Since you also stay at the inn, I'm looking forward to it," Max added, "Sarah?"

At first, Liz, forgetting she was Sarah, didn't respond.

Then, she remembered, "Yes." *Now is the time to tell him my real name.*

"It's nice meeting an honest woman."

Liz wanted to crawl into a hole. Now was not the time! She opted to confess later.

They enjoyed the ride through the town, looking at the giant ornamental holiday balls in red and green decorating each street corner. Holly and ivy partnered with strands of blinking white lights everywhere. Since it had snowed last night, the children made snowmen and enjoyed snowball fights. The clouds created an overcast, so the holiday-colored lights glistened all over the storefronts. It looked as if Christmas had exploded throughout the town.

Liz slowed down for Max to see the view. She wanted him to experience the warmth of the town. He demonstrated a sweet spirit. Like Liz, he was fascinated by the snow and holiday lights.

When they stopped at a streetlight, Liz pointed toward the park. "That huge Christmas tree in the central park is decorated by the local high school senior class. It's been a tradition for over fifty years. The townspeople gather for a formal lighting ceremony the first weekend of December."

"That's a great custom."

"The community gathers the weekend before Christmas and sings carols in front of the pavilion. White carriages stationed near the benches on the park's west side are available as long as people wait in line. The rides usually last about thirty minutes, travel through every park, and make people feel as if they are in a romantic movie."

"What about the red carriages?"

"They offer rides through the top three neighborhoods with the best decorations and the smaller parks decorated by the civic clubs. The red carriages run from six until eleven o'clock."

Temporarily, Liz forgot about her big lie. Talking about the carriages brought a memory of Jake. He was the last person to take her on a buggy ride. The night before he left town, he reserved a horse-drawn carriage. Now that she recalled that evening, Jake may have planned to announce his new decision that didn't include her, but he never had the opportunity or didn't have the courage.

"I'd like to see the town by carriage ride as long as I have warm blankets," said Max.

Liz hoped Max would invite her for a ride sometime this week. She was surprised at her reaction to that idea, which would provide another chance to tell him about the lie. She couldn't confess now; she didn't want to spoil the moment. Max interrupted Liz's thinking and resolved her dilemma.

"Where are the ski slopes located?" asked Max.

"You must go to Concord for skiing. A bus to the slopes is available every thirty minutes, and it is free for guests at both hotels.

The local college drama department presents a Wellington Christmas on Ice the four days before Christmas Eve. I recommend shopping on Tuesday because it's the designated day for guests at both hotels, and everybody is at the show."

"I'll remember that. How come you know all this information about this town?"

"You should have received the events envelope from The Bradford Inn. Did you?"

"I'm sure the package went to my dad's house in Orlando."

"There's a Welcome to Wellington brochure that includes the town history. It's from the chamber of commerce. Please read it. It's great."

When Liz pulled in front of the inn, she looked at Deep Voice to see his reaction. Max looked at the grand building and glanced toward the business sign to ensure the structure he saw was The Bradford Inn.

"It's beautiful! It doesn't even look like the same place. And you are staying here, too?"

Liz beamed. "Yes, I'm sure I will see you around."

"I hope so. Maybe we can have lunch or something."

"I would like that."

"Great! Thanks again for the ride."

Max couldn't think. Sitting in Sarah's car, he was surprised he wasn't frustrated about this place. Instead, Max felt as if he was on a new adventure, and it was because of Miss Emerald Eyes. He looked forward to staying here. Max exited the car, grabbed his suitcase from the back seat, and headed to the entrance. He didn't notice the cold wind as it blew in his face.

As Max approached the entrance, "I forgot to get her phone number. How could I fail to remember an essential piece of information like that? Shoot, I don't even know her last name!" He focused. The signs were apparent: no last name, no phone number. He must get those emerald eyes out of his brain. *Remember my mantra!*

He stopped and shook his head. As he glimpsed at the front porch, his mind did not think about his fiasco wedding but only the bright green eyes of a spunky, auburn-haired lady. *Maybe I need to get to know my new friend while here. How difficult will it be to find a beautiful woman named Sarah?*

As he opened the massive doors, Max said, “This may be the most memorable Christmas ever!”

When Max entered the lobby, he was encouraged by the possibilities. He admired the beauty of the room. Happy elves and elaborate ornaments hung from tables and lighting fixtures. Life-size wooden soldiers greeted guests at the entrance, the corridors, and by the staircase to the mezzanine. Garland, with blinking lights, followed the railings to the second-floor café. The beauty of Christmas was everywhere.

As he perused the guests in the lobby, he recognized his mother, Jill, and his sister, Marty Woodson. Max watched as his family admired the unusual decorations on the Christmas tree in the center circle of the marble floor, hoping Sarah would enter the lobby. He wanted to introduce her to his relatives.

He was about to say hello when a woman standing by Marty turned and smiled coyly at him. Max stared. Standing like a porcelain doll in front of the tall holiday tree was someone he had no desire to see. *What is my ex-wife, Becca, doing here?*

Chapter 5

For an awkward moment, no one moved. Realizing Max would not advance toward them, Jill, followed by Marty, approached him. He hugged his mother and sister. The third person waited for Max to speak, but he refused. Instead, he ignored Becca.

"Max, my sweetheart, I understand this is quite a surprise for you, but I thought about this elegant place and returned to our special inn this Christmas, too. It was wonderful to see your family when I arrived."

Max focused on his mother and sister, waiting for an explanation. Becca was the last person he expected to see in the hotel. Finally, Jill grabbed Max by the arm and tried to save the situation.

Mother piped in, "This is such a big coincidence."

"It was a huge surprise to find Becca here," added Marty.

Quietly to Max, Jill commented, "I understand it is a shock to see her, but maybe something good will come of this situation."

Max whispered, "For the record, I am happy in my work and my single life."

Jill spoke softly in Max's ear. "You think you are happy. We know better."

In shock at what he heard, Max approached the front desk to register. He was at a loss for words and needed to avoid conniving, lying Becca. He was glad his honest, sweet Sarah did not follow him into the hotel.

When Jill realized where Max was heading, she grabbed his arm. “Max, Becca has a small issue.”

“What?”

“When Becca tried to check in today, there was a problem with her reservation. There were no rooms left.”

Max yelled, “I don’t have a room?”

Jill responded quietly, “No, Son, you have a room. Becca doesn’t. The inn lost her booking!”

Max glared at his calculating ex-wife standing there like a family member, arm in arm with Marty. He figured Becca was behind all of this. His mother and Marty had no clue.

For a moment, he looked around at the renovations of The Bradford Inn. Everything was new. How was he going to fix this situation? Becca knew Max would not make a scene and embarrass his mother. Every time Max tried to focus, his mind thought about sweet Sarah. This holiday trip to The Bradford Inn included a lady with emerald eyes, and Max looked forward to seeing her again. What was he going to do?

Max's smile returned for the first time in the last few minutes. He knew exactly what to do! Becca’s game plan was about to implode.

Jill and Marty misread the expression on Max’s face. They assumed Max would solve the issue and allow Becca to stay in his suite. There was no other option for the poor girl who had no place to sleep.

Max addressed his mother.“Becca can find another hotel or go home. A train departs in two hours. She has plenty of time to catch it.”

Max turned abruptly and moved toward the registration desk. All three women, shocked at the turn of events, followed him. They whispered among themselves. He wrote a brief note on The Bradford Inn notepad at the desk. After folding the message, he wrote on top and handed it to the clerk.

“Would you see a guest named Sarah receives this note? I don’t know her last name, but she is registering soon, I think. This information is important. I have a reservation. I’m Maxwell Harvelle.”

The clerk could not locate a guest named Sarah on the registration list. Max told him it was probably because the lady was parking her car. He completed his check-in process and headed for the elevators.

As he turned to leave, he reminded the clerk, "Please save that note for Sarah. She will be checking in soon."

Max glanced at scheming Becca, who stood nearby. "Have a safe trip."

Marty appealed to her brother, "Max? We have a situation here. We can't leave Becca stranded."

Max knew he couldn't allow Becca to stay in his suite; Sarah would never understand that. Max paused, "Well, aren't you registered here?"

"Yes."

Max glanced toward his mother. "Are you, too?"

"Of course."

Max spoke gently to his mom. "All rooms here are suites that include a TV room with a large sofa. I suggest one of you invite her to stay with you."

Both Marty and Jill gasped.

Becca quickly questioned, "Max?"

Max turned and stepped into the elevator.

"Merry Christmas, Becca." Max looked at his watch. "If a room is unavailable, the train leaves in an hour and forty-five minutes."

The three women were appalled but exercised restraint when elevator number one closed in front of them. Elevator number two opened, and Liz stepped out as three stunned women entered.

Marty whispered, "Mom, do we have a plan B?"

Annabelle Bradford began her workday every morning in her office by preparing a pot of coffee and checking her schedule for the day. Wearing a red business pantsuit, she enjoyed her coffee and updated her plans. The lady sat at a massive brown desk designed by Uncle James Bradford, who had begun the hotel business about fifty years ago.

The room, surrounded by matching bookcases on three walls, framed her as she worked. On the fourth wall was the portrait of James Bradford. Next to it was a matching picture of Annabelle's husband, Lawrence. She claimed her success was due to the times she conferred with the portraits and made decisions based on their leadership styles.

This week, a deep pink Christmas cactus decorated the left corner of her desk. Annabelle was a beautiful lady and worked long hours to continue the family's legacy. At five feet ten inches, she maintained a slim physique. Her leadership skills built a strong employee team. She listened to suggestions and never took credit for someone else's ideas. She created a sense of a family work environment.

Annabelle's cell phone rang. Recognizing the cell phone number, she took the call. "Hello. Jake. I'm glad you called. Is everything arranged with Sam for tomorrow night?"

"Yes, your sound system is spectacular! I'm impressed."

"That's what our guest performers claim. Glad you are happy with it. I must give credit to Liz. She selected the system."

"That's why I'm calling. Is Lizzie back? I want to talk to her."

"She returns today, but I have not seen her yet."

"Please give her my message about the meeting."

"I told Liz last night on the phone."

"Great. Please ask her to remember to call me when she gets into the office. Thanks. Bye."

After the call to The Bradford Inn, Jake sat in his suite, reviewing his plan to approach Lizzie. He had made a big mistake when he had left town the day after high school graduation. He should have explained his decision to her, but he had not wanted to admit that he would never pass a class in college. If Lizzie hadn't helped him with the answers to most of his homework, Jake would not have graduated from high school.

Jake moved to the window in his bedroom and studied the children playing in the park across the street. The award-winning singer was in trouble now. If this next album didn't sell, every record company would ignore him. Jake Jones was desperate for endorsements, investors, and Lizzie's money.

He made a cup of coffee and grabbed a donut from the bag he had purchased at the hotel cafe. He returned to the big chair in his room and reviewed the steps in his plan.

First, he had to apologize and beg for forgiveness. He would skip practice and spend some time with his old classmate. Then, he would get down on one knee and ask Lizzie to marry him. Chicks loved that romantic crap.

He'd control the bank account just like he had done when they had gigs in high school. Five days with Lizzie was all he needed. He planned to cut the holiday short after their wedding, return to Nashville, and cut the album. Afterward, Jake would hit the road for a long tour. *Oh, the enormous sacrifices a person must make to be a success.*

Jake grabbed another donut. *Thank you, Lizzie, for being the lamb!*

Jake made a sad face and then cracked up.

Chapter 6

When Liz entered the hotel lounge, she found Sam, the bartender, cleaning the counter. The advertisement outside the door displayed a big picture of Jake. Remembering how Max admired Vermont's country music star's music, she considered reserving tickets for the concert.

"Welcome home. Was it a successful trip?"

"Yes, it was." Liz hugged Sam, her long-time friend.

"I knew you could do it. Proud of you."

Sam, who was in his fifties, was a handsome man and always wore a white shirt, a bow tie, a black vest, and black pants. Everybody loved him because he was friendly. However, patrons mainly loved Sam because he listened and held confidences. He knew all the secrets.

"Hey, where is your royal blue bow tie that matches those eyes?" asked Liz.

"I've switched to red for Christmas."

"I love it."

"I knew you would."

"I need six tickets for the concert tonight."

"You are buying six tickets to a Jake Jones concert?"

"They're not for me, Sam. I am going to give them away. Can you arrange for my guests to have a front-row table?"

Sam looked carefully at Liz, concerned about her state of mind. "Sure. What name should I write on the reserved seats?"

"Max."

"Max who?"

Liz fidgeted. "Well, I don't know his last name."

Sam laid his pencil on the bar and gave all his attention to Liz.

"Don't give me that look, Sam. I met him on the train yesterday. His family is celebrating Christmas here."

"Okay, got it covered." Sam asked, "Is this stranger married?"

"Divorced."

"Divorced, with children?"

"What does that have to do with anything?"

"I'm just asking."

"He didn't mention any children." Liz rolled her eyes.

"That would be important to Annabelle." Sam looked down, then up, and winked at Liz.

"Oh my gosh! You're crazy."

"You must like this stranger since you're buying six concert tickets."

"He is not a stranger. He's a nice guy, and he loves Jake Jones."

Sam grinned and wiped the counter. "Something doesn't jive here."

"What?" asked Liz.

"You're attracted to a man who loves Jake Jones. You despise that singer. Your future marriage is doomed. Oh, I forgot. You don't know Max's last name?"

"I didn't say I was attracted to him!"

"I read you like a book!" Sam placed glasses on the bar rack.

"Sam!"

"Yes."

"Let's return to the subject of concert tickets."

"Sure, those tickets are thirty dollars each. Credit card or cash?"

"Cash."

"Okay, that will be $180. Tell me about your trip. If you wish, you can leave out the part about meeting the cute guy with no last name and no children."

"Sam!"

"Yes." Sam handed her a bottle of water after she gave him the cash.

"You need to forget Max." Liz took a deep breath. "My trip was productive. Five new conferences booked for next year."

"Wow! Does Annabelle know?"

"Yeah, but not about Max, and I would like it to remain that way."

"Okay, your secret is safe with me." Sam said, "I'm not to tell Annabelle you are attracted to someone named Max whom you met on the train, and you don't know his last name or if he has children. Are you planning to elope?"

"You realize you are making fun of the current VP of marketing!"

"Absolutely," Sam responded in a lighthearted mood. "Did I mention grandchild number two is on the way? A daughter this time."

"Mrs. Annabelle hit me with that news last night on the phone. In the future, would you please not announce any new babies until their birth? That gives my mother another nine months to harass her children." Liz was happy for Sam. "Congratulations! Have you started purchasing toys yet?"

"We purchased a soft, cuddly baby doll yesterday. Also, Jake asked me to tell you he wants to see you before the concert tonight."

Liz looked away from Sam. "Consider the message delivered. I refuse to meet him." She accidentally turned over her bottle of water.

"He is adamant about seeing you this time. He asked for your phone number." Sam wiped the counter and handed another bottle to Liz

"You didn't…"

"I didn't give it to him."

"Thank you. Why did you let Mother sign that nut for the holiday entertainment? He will be around here looking for me for five days."

"Annabelle brought the signed contracts into my office. Never discussed it with me."

"I anticipated a nice, relaxing holiday this year. Now, I must dodge the man who dumped me." Liz placed her head in her hands. "Sam?"

"Huh?"

"Please keep Jake away from me."

"I will do what I can."

After reviewing the arrangements for that night's concert, Liz left the bar and walked down the corridor toward the registration area. She enjoyed the Christmas music and examined the holiday decorations. She trusted Sam. He was not only the manager of the lounge but her dear friend.

Liz had learned that Sam was an excellent negotiator when Liz and her mother argued over colors, policy, and strategies. Liz referred to her college training, and Annabelle relied on instinct. Both presented their ideas to Sam, who offered a recommendation. His skill in arbitration prevented arguments between Liz and her mother.

Usually, Sam managed the lounge, and Liz oversaw the entertainment. When Liz was promoted to VP of Marketing, Sam assumed the responsibilities of everything related to the nightclub, which left Liz free to travel and increase the inn's client base. However, Liz enjoyed working with him and never relinquished her role when scheduling concerts. Liz and Sam made a great team.

She trusted the bartender and discussed business ideas with him before sharing them with Annabelle. She considered him her big uncle. She knew he would keep Jake away, if possible.

When Liz arrived at the front desk, the clerk was on break. When she checked the computer for Max's name, she was thankful only one Max was registered. She located his room number and wrote a brief message inviting him to tonight's performance. Liz left instructions on how to get the tickets. She signed the note, **Sarah**.

There was that lie again. Liz had never told Max her real name while traveling from the train station. She rationalized they were excited about the Christmas decorations and the snow flurries. After placing the message on the clerk's desk for the note to be delivered ASAP, she walked to the restaurant to see her mother. *I could call his room and tell him the truth. No, that's not a good idea. It should be face-to-face. That's more personal. I will explain tonight when he arrives at the concert.*

When the clerk returned to the front desk, he saw the note from Sarah to Max. The clerk remembered the earlier card to Sarah from Max and looked for it in the basket. When he found the original message, he rechecked the hotel registration list and found no one named Sarah.

The clerk rang the service bell. "Please deliver this note to Mr. Maxwell in suite number 224 and return to the main desk immediately. Something strange is going on."

After delivering the message, the bellhop walked to the main desk. "Note delivered to suite number 224, Sir."

"Listen, we have a lady named Sarah staying at the inn. However, she has neither registered nor paid for her lodging."

"What does she look like?"

"Not a clue! Listen for the name Sarah. If you find her, let me know. It is a confidential matter and of utmost importance."

"Did I tell you I'm a criminology major?"

"Yes, many times."

This year, the bellhop had enrolled at the local college because he was undecided about his future. He had discovered his course in crime studies was exciting and had vowed to become a private investigator or possibly to work for the FBI.

In high school, he had preferred playing video games instead of studying. However, he had regretted that decision in his first year at the post-secondary level. He hadn't enjoyed the general education classes and had felt they wasted his time. But that criminology class had inspired him. Now, all he wanted to do was solve a big case.

"Just call me Sherlock!"

"Huh? Are you okay?" asked the clerk, who stood with his arms crossed.

"Yes, I'm just reviewing the facts, Sir."

The clerk paused before staring at the young employee. "I hesitate to say this, but follow your instincts and find the missing Sarah."

The bellhop saluted. "I'm on it."

The criminology major went to his employee lounge locker and placed a small notebook in his pocket. "My first investigation case. Find a woman named Sarah - no last name. No description. That shouldn't be too difficult for a smart sleuthhound like me."

Liz found her mother talking to the hotel florist about the table decorations in the dining hall. Liz admired the holiday embellishments as she entered and realized how special this place was to its guests, especially at Christmas. Her mother was an unbelievably detailed lady who wanted every table unique for the guests each night.

Annabelle looked affectionately at her daughter as she proceeded into the dining hall. Liz looked cute in her outfit and showed liveliness in her walk. The boss assumed her little girl had talked to Jake. If Annabelle was correct, a wedding was in the future, and grandchildren would follow. She made the right decision when she gave the job to her baby's high school sweetheart.

This Christmas was the third year the family had run the hotel, and the business had tripled due to Liz's ideas. Annabelle was skeptical when Liz had changed her major to business administration rather than music, but it was the best decision for both the inn and Liz. She poured a cup of hot tea for herself and handed a bottle of water to Liz. They sat at a small dining table to discuss the new contracts.

Annabelle brought Jake Jones into the conversation. "Listen, he has a following. People from town purchased half of the tickets for tonight and Saturday."

"Huh, I don't see how he can be so popular. He can't sing solo."

"He is debuting new songs for his next album." Annabelle added, "That might bring national attention to our inn."

"Maybe I need to invite the local news," Liz suggested.

"Jake has already contacted them."

"I hope our guests enjoy country music."

"I'm glad to hear you say that, Sweetheart. I believe Jake has changed."

"Was it your idea to offer the gig or his?"

"Now that I remember, he came into my office, looking for you, as I ended my phone call with the quartet. It was a coincidence."

"But he offered to help you out, didn't he?"

"It was his idea, but I would have asked him anyway after my conversation. His attitude is different. I think he's more responsible now. Success has given Jake confidence."

"Good." Liz took some comfort from her mother's assertion, but she wasn't sure she believed it.

"And he gave us a deal," Annabelle said. "He dropped his usual performance fee."

"What are we paying him?"

"The same as the quartet."

Liz's brows arched upward. "Really?"

"I want you to think about talking to him. He seems down to earth. He's not self-centered as you would expect a superstar to be." Annabelle hoped Liz would admit that she and Jake had met.

But Liz didn't voice her doubts aloud. Now was not the time for an argument. "Listen, I have some gifts to buy. I'll be in and out of my office until after Christmas. Okay?"

"After what you accomplished on this trip?" Annabelle beamed with pride at her daughter's accomplishments. "Absolutely. Take a few days and enjoy the snow."

"Text me if you need me."

"I will," Annabelle assured her. "Are you, by any chance, going to the concert tonight?"

"No, that loud music hurts my ears. But I will stop by for a few songs while Jake is here. I don't see how Sam keeps his hearing with all that loud music each week."

"Liz, please give that man a chance."

To avoid further discussion about Jake, Liz reviewed the new contracts. Annabelle had questions but found everything in order. They talked about personnel issues, and Liz remembered the sweet man she had met on the train.

She kissed her mom and headed out of the dining room and toward the front desk in the lobby. Liz could not stop smiling when she thought of her new friend. Max would be thrilled when he received those tickets to the concert. He was a sweetheart. Her mom was still pushing that country singer on her. *What's his name?* Liz laughed.

Annabelle watched her daughter walk away and again noticed Liz appeared to have a little pep in her step. Liz is happy about something, and it's because Jake apologized to her. *Why won't she tell me? Could it be my Christmas present? That's it. Their marriage will be the best gift of all. Won't it be wonderful if they announce their engagement?*

Annabelle created an immediate plan for a party for the whole town. The restaurant would be perfect for the event. She assumed many of Jake's famous friends would attend. Tears filled her eyes. Her baby was getting married to her high school sweetheart.

While exiting the meeting with her mom, Liz called Sam. When he answered the phone, Liz stepped aside and asked Sam to reserve a table in the front row, center, if possible. Sam confirmed he had booked most tables but would change the chart to accommodate her special guests.

"Anything to save your love life," Sam teased.

Liz cleared her throat. "Max will pick up the tickets from you. His last name is Harvelle, and he may mention the name 'Sarah.' Max doesn't know my real name yet."

"You played the name game with this guy?" Sam asked.

"I didn't know he was a nice person at the time I introduced myself."

"It sounds like your relationship with this 'Max' is a little rocky at this point. You need to tell him your real name."

"Sam?"

"Yes?"

"I am not in a relationship yet."

"Gotcha. You bought six tickets for a total stranger."

"Are you expecting a present from me this holiday season?"

"A big one. I know something about you that Annabelle wants to know. Bye."

Liz remembered the gift she had ordered for Sam. *I may buy him a red nose to wear on that clown face!*

The holiday music created a warm and friendly atmosphere at the inn. Liz arrived at the main desk, where the clerk was busy talking with someone who had issues with accommodations. She quickly wrote Max another note about the reserved table for his family. She signed the message from **Sarah** and dropped it in the brown wicker basket. *Sam's right; I will reveal my name tonight.*

Humming the holiday music, she headed for elevator number two. She imagined Max's beautiful eyes would shine with exhilaration when he read that she had reserved a front-row table. Max Harvelle was a VIP to her.

Jake Jones passed by the front desk as the elevator doors closed. He was heading toward the corridor. Liz caught a glimpse of him and moved to the elevator's corner out of his vision. It was time for Liz to disappear.

When the bellhop checked the basket at the main desk, he saw the note for Max. He headed toward the elevator to deliver it to the second floor. The bellhop made a memo in his notebook. **Max knows Sarah.**

The bellhop looked everywhere for the missing Sarah. She was very clever. However, he had studied to be a detective, as in the movies. Sarah was no match for the confident sleuth. He excelled in his methods. *I must memorize the Minerva Rights to read them to Sarah when I handcuff her. I wonder where I can find shackles?*

Chapter 7

Later as Jill, Marty, and Becca entered the hotel lounge, they were thankful no other patrons were present. The ladies sat away from the entrance, near the bar. The group needed to collaborate and redesign their plan.

When Sam approached their table, Jill asked for water and said they had stopped by for a short conference. She asked Sam for permission.

Sam responded, "No problem. Stay as long as you like."

"Thank you!" Marty spoke as Sam returned to the bar area.

Jill asked, "Did you see the sign? Jake Jones is here in concert tonight?"

"Yeah, I wonder if Max knows?" asked Marty.

"Why would Max care about him?" asked Becca. "Jake Jones can't sing."

"Max listens to that singer daily."

"Oh, I don't believe it. A country-western singer? Good grief, Max has been in those woods too long!" squawked Becca.

Marty and Jill looked at each other.

"Becca, your reconnection is not going as planned," Jill began the meeting.

While Becca remained quiet, Marty realized she should have asked more questions when Becca called them on Thanksgiving Day and hinted about a new relationship between Max and her.

Sam returned to the table with water for the ladies.

Jill asked, “Where can we buy tickets for the Jake Jones concert for tonight’s show?”

“Here, but Friday and Saturday night performances are sold out. I have seats left for Monday and Tuesday.”

“What do you think? Should we buy tickets?” asked Jill, looking at her daughter.

Marty advised, “Let’s wait on Dad and Charlie. They may want to go, too.”

“Thanks. We will wait on our husbands before we make a decision.”

“Okay, I’m Sam. See me for the tickets.”

“Okay, thank you.”

Jill waited for Sam to return to the bar. “Back to the purpose of our meeting.”

“When was the last time you contacted Max?” questioned Marty.

Becca was careful with her answers. “I’ve tried several times to revitalize our relationship over the last few years.”

Jill asked, “But did you actually talk about it with Max?”

“We conversed several times. I believe that’s why he never married. He was waiting for me to make the first step toward reconciliation.”

“What did Max say that led you to believe he wanted to remarry?” asked Jill.

“It wasn’t what he said. It was the sound in his voice. He is lonely and never fell in love with anyone, which was the biggest sign.”

Marty and Jill glanced at each other and then toward Becca. Marty asked, “Were there any other signs that he was interested in a new relationship?”

“Of course,” answered Becca as she shifted in her chair. “Uh, he didn’t object to the idea.”

The ladies paused as they contemplated what to do next since Max was not following Jill’s plan.

“We must think about what to do now. Does anyone have any ideas?” asked Marty as she observed Becca.

The ladies brainstormed ideas about getting Max and Becca on the same page. After much discussion, Jill formulated Plan B to get

Max to talk to Becca. The ladies were too busy strategizing and did not see the hotel bellhop enter and sit quietly eating a bag lunch.

"Tonight, Marty and I will leave the restaurant early after dinner. That will leave you alone with Max," said Jill.

Marty added, "You will have the opportunity to talk about your differences and see if he is receptive to spending time with you. After the conversation, invite him to come here to the lounge. The show doesn't start until eight. Have a drink and then when you leave, call Mom and provide an update."

Becca nodded her head. "Okay."

"What if she isn't successful?" asked Marty, chewing her thumbnail.

"We'll meet in my suite and figure something out," said Jill. "Dad doesn't know about our plan."

"I've also kept my husband in the dark as a precaution."

"I think it's best we keep this mission between us. If our spouses begin to ask questions, the whole situation may blow up in our faces."

Becca assured them, "I have this. I won't screw it up. I know how to do it."

"I hope it works," responded Marty. "We don't have that much time left."

"If we fail this time," Becca admitted, "I have a plan C, also. I think I will change into an appropriate outfit for the job."

As Becca left the lounge, none of the ladies noticed the bellhop exiting the room. He had heard the last part of the conversation.

Jill looked at Marty. "When Becca called before Thanksgiving, weren't you under the impression she and Max were talking to each other?"

"Yes, I thought they were all but officially engaged. But I never asked Max about it. I was afraid to mention it. I expected him to tell us, but he never did."

Jill remembered how Max never mentioned anything regarding Becca, either. "And he did not want to come to Vermont for Christmas."

Marty interrupted, "When Dad and my husband arrive tomorrow afternoon, Charlie won't be happy about Becca sleeping in our suite all week."

"Dan will inform Becca to exit the room immediately. I must convince Max to take her in. I will wait until he and Becca talk before I beg my son for a favor. That solves one problem."

"But Max may kill us if Becca stays in his room."

Jill agreed. "There is that option. The good news is Dan and Charlie are not arriving until tomorrow. We have time to get this situation resolved."

Jill watched Max enter the lounge. "Look who is here? Are you searching for us?"

Max said, "No, I'm here to pick up tickets for the Jake Jones concert tonight."

"The concert is sold out tonight and Saturday. How did you get tickets?"

Max informed his mother, "I know people."

Jill and Marty looked at each other and laughed. "Yeah, in low places."

"You must be careful what you say about your favorite son and brother."

"I have only one son."

Max hugged his mom. "Let me talk to a person named Sam, and I'll sit with you."

"Sam is the guy behind there." Marty pointed to the bar.

"How do you know Sam?"

Marty answered, "We know the names of all the bartenders in the area. We have been here for a few days. Remember?"

Both ladies waited and watched as Max talked to the bartender. A huge smile flashed across Max's face.

Jill said, "Something is going on."

Marty agreed. "Yes, I wonder why Max is that excited."

Max grinned as he waited for Sam to retrieve the concert tickets. His life couldn't be better. Becca was gone from the inn. He would see Sarah tonight, and now, a front-row reserved table at the Jake Jones concert. He felt the Christmas spirit.

When Max returned to Jill and Marty, he asked, "Guess what?"

Marty asked, "What?"

"Not only do I have tickets to the sold-out concert, but I also have a reserved table in front of Jake Jones — the best seats in the house."

"How much did that cost you?" asked Marty.

"Nothing. I am a VIP!"

"How many tickets did you get?" asked Marty.

"Enough for my family and a guest. Six!"

"But Dad and Charlie won't be here tonight. They're flying out tomorrow."

"Heck, I forgot that. I'll see if I can exchange two tickets for tomorrow night."

"Sam told us tickets were sold out for tomorrow night, too." Jill hated that Dan and Charlie would miss the show.

"Don't forget I am a VIP. I'll talk to the ticket man."

"Don't be too disappointed, Son,"

They watched Max approach Sam. Sam laughed and exchanged the tickets. Jill and Marty looked at each other.

When Max returned to the table with the exchanged tickets in his hand, Jill asked, "How did you get tickets for a sold-out concert?"

"As I said, 'I have connections.'"

All three laughed and agreed to meet at six in the lobby for dinner.

The bellhop watched from behind one of the columns as the group left the lounge together. Mr. Max split from the ladies and went another way. The future criminologist examined his notes. **Ladies have a plan, and spouses are mentioned. Pretty lady – the perpetrator, older lady - the gang leader.** *I wish I had sat nearer the group. I could not hear them very well. This evidence proves anyone can commit a crime. I also see an A in my future and the distinguished service award.* "Do they give the Congressional Medal of Honor to a young person like me?"

The ladies were talking and never noticed the bellhop hiding behind the column. When he moved to follow them, the bellhop did not see the Do Not Enter sign for the seating area near the exterior wall. Earlier, a guest had had an accident and had spilled a pot of coffee on the tiled floor. When the bellhop tiptoed to the next column, he stepped into the coffee spatter and slid feet first under the olive green, nineteenth-century sofa, bouncing into the wall. But the boy held his evidence notebook high in the air as he glided across the waxed surface.

Jill and Marty, focused on executing their plan, never heard the commotion of the messy bellhop sliding into the hotel furniture.

"Marty, are you thinking the same thing I am thinking?" asked Jill as they walked toward the elevators.

"If that extra ticket is for Becca, then yes."

"I don't know how he got those tickets, but he planned one for Becca. That is obvious."

"I believe in my heart that we did the right thing by bringing those two together." Marty put her arm around her mother as they entered the elevator.

An hour later, someone knocked on Jill Harvelle's door. When she opened it, she screamed.

Recognizing the gang leader, the bellhop dropped the luggage and ran to stand in front of Dan Harvelle, the husband of Jill, to protect him from an assault from the female standing in the doorway.

"Ma'am, according to our records, this gentleman claims to be your husband. Do you wish to press charges against this perpetrator for stealing your husband's identity?" The bellhop gasped for breath as he pressed Dan back from the door.

"That's my husband!" Jill shouted.

"Frankly, Darling, this is not the reception I anticipated!"

"I'm sorry. You're not supposed to be here until tomorrow. What do you expect?" She grabbed her husband and hugged him.

"I wanted to surprise you."

"Well, you did that! I need to sit down and think. In the future, tell me when you plan to surprise me."

The bellhop turned around and looked at Dan, who was shaking his head. "Sir, does your wife usually scream when she sees you?"

"Young man, only when she is up to something." Dan winked at the bellhop.

The bellhop delivered the luggage inside the suite and quickly canvassed the living area, looking for anything unusual. *This is a strange situation I am investigating. Oh!* The bellhop hurriedly backed out of the room when he saw the other tall, beautiful woman leaning against the bedroom door frame. He had to document what he had witnessed. *Oh my, the plot thickens!*

Dan entered the suite and turned toward the bedroom. There, standing against the doorframe of the bedroom, was Becca. He looked at his wife and waited.

Jill began, "I know this is a shock, but Becca chose to return to the same hotel this year. What a coincidence! We were having coffee and getting re-acquainted."

Dan asked, "Does Max know you are here?"

"Yes, we met earlier and talked." Becca stretched the truth.

"I'm glad to hear that. I think I will take a shower and get ready for dinner. The meal on the plane was terrible, and I'm starving. Becca, will you be dining with us tonight?"

"I hope so."

"Well, if it doesn't work out, good seeing you."

While Dan bathed, Jill adapted plan B. She texted Marty the new steps to follow. "Becca, you go shopping or something. Marty will text you when she and Charlie are leaving their suite. You dress quickly for the evening and join us at the restaurant. After dinner, when you and Max arrive at the lounge, give us a thumbs up if everything is going well. Got that?"

"Yes."

"Everything else is the same plan. Okay?"

"Yes, I got it."

Jill's scheme was falling apart because her loving husband showed up a day early. "You'll have time to dress for dinner. The plan is still a go, but it is a little more complicated now that our husbands arrived early."

"I got this."

"Oh, I forgot. Max has a ticket for you for the Jake Jones concert tonight."

"He does? That's wonderful."

"We are all going. Oh no, Max exchanged Dan and Charlie's tickets. I must call Max. You plan to go to the concert after dinner. Go! Go! Before Dan finishes his bath. I must call Max and tell him to get two tickets back."

Jill ushered Becca out the door and called Max.

While Jill checked her make-up, Dan asked, "I am concerned about the coincidence with Becca returning here at the same time our family is here. Is there anything I need to know about that situation?"

"Everything is fine. I knew Becca might be here, and Max met her when he arrived."

Dan walked toward his wife and kissed her. "I have missed you this week."

Jill adjusted her husband's tie. "And I missed you. I'm glad you arrived tonight because Max has a surprise for you."

"What is it?"

"I'll wait and let him tell you."

"Before I forget, thanks for those frozen casseroles you left for Charlie and me. We ate every one of them. Charlie was so lonely without Marty; he slept in our guest bedroom all week."

"Really?" Jill reflected on the past week. "They seem to be closer. Marty called him several times a day."

"It was Charlie's idea to catch an early flight. We took our luggage to work today."

"How is everything at the bank?"

"Good. Charlie had a banner quarter. He acquired more investors this year than any producer."

"That's good news."

"He will receive a great bonus check this year."

"And as the president of the bank, that makes you very happy, doesn't it?"

"Very happy." Dan kissed his wife again. "Let's go meet the others. I'm hungry and want to know my surprise."

"Okay."

Thirty minutes later, Christmas music entertained the Harvelle family as they strolled toward the restaurant, planned for walks in the snow, repeated old stories, and bragged about college football. They discussed the Jake Jones concert, thankful Max could exchange the tickets again, making Dan and Charlie happy. The two women in the family group disguised their anxiety as they planned to make Max a happy man.

Becca, glad for an excuse to be away from the happy Harvelle family, headed to the café for coffee and to regroup. She was frustrated with having to smile continuously and to act friendly with strangers. Five years had changed Max. She assumed he would be kinder, but he was different and more assertive! There's no girlfriend with him.

She remembered how hard she had had to work to get him interested in her in the first place. Considering Jill's plan, Becca refocused and changed the outfit she had planned to wear tonight. Yes, that red outfit would definitely get his full attention. *And he bought me a ticket to the concert.*

After receiving a text, Becca returned to Marty's suite; the holiday music in the hallway interrupted her thinking. Somebody needed to shut that noise off; she was sick of those tacky jingles. Becca sneered. The next time Max saw her in that red dress, he wouldn't be able to resist her. *I got this!*

Becca was born into a family of educators. She had borrowed heavily to attend an elite university, looking for a rich husband. In her junior year, when she had discovered Max was the son of the president of the biggest bank in Orlando, Becca latched on to him immediately. She had made sure she was perfect in every way.

When Max had announced that he was moving to rural Madison County to create his own company about six weeks after their wedding, Becca had laughed. She had thought he was joking. Thinking she would change his mind, she had moved with him and had played the game, hoping he would become bored and return to the city in a few months.

Instead, Max had loved the serenity of the small town, but Becca had hated it. When she had asked for a divorce, she had thought he would not agree to that situation and would follow her to save their marriage. He did not.

After four years of hunting a rich man, Becca was impoverished. She had difficulty keeping a job. She had beauty but no occupational skills. She had met a con artist who made off with most of the money left to her by her grandfather's small estate.

With no funds and no job, she was desperate. As a last resort, Becca had devised a plan to reconnect with Max. She had hoped he would give her money to help her transition to her new career. She needed start-up dollars for her new company. Her ploy was perfect.

The first phase had begun before Thanksgiving when Becca conned Jill and Marty with a reconciliation scenario. Next, Becca had planned to convince Max to help her with her new business venture. Then, she would move on and build her empire. If that failed, she would resort to the least desirable alternative.

Collaboration with Jill and Marty was brilliant. They loved Max so much they would make this plan happen. Tonight, Becca would look like a million dollars. During the meal, she would schedule a conference with Max to convince him to invest in her vision. She crossed her fingers and hoped she didn't have to marry him to get the money.

Chapter 8

After Max and his family were seated at the restaurant, a bell rang. From the center back area, a curtain lifted toward the ceiling. A chef dressed in black stood on a rolling stage that proceeded forward with the main course served on a huge table. Annabelle approached the microphone. She held a beautiful, decorative Christmas ball in her right hand.

Annabelle, wearing a beautiful red brocade dress, greeted her guests. "Before we begin dinner, I want to draw your attention to our annual scavenger hunt starting tomorrow at 9:00 a.m. We have placed Christmas ornaments like this one (holding it up for the guests to view) in three discreet hiding places in or outside the inn. Three balls have numbers on them. If the number is one or two, the prize is $500 to the person who finds them first."

The audience reacted and applauded. Everyone loved the idea and shared where they would begin searching.

Then Annabelle got their attention again. "Whoever finds the decoration with the number three will receive $1,000."

The audience came back again with louder applause.

Annabelle continued, "Beware! There are decoy Christmas balls with no numbers on them."

The audience replied, "Ahhh." Laughter trickled through the crowd.

Annabelle consoled them, "When you find a decoy, head to the restaurant. A special treat will be here for you and up to three guests.

When you find a numbered ornament, please take it to the main desk in the lobby. We hope everyone participates. Have fun, and Merry Christmas from The Bradford Inn!"

The audience applauded loudly again.

Annabelle concluded, "Now, welcome to our Friday night feast prepared by Chef Miguel. Enjoy."

Becca, who had arrived during the middle of Annabelle's speech, remained at the entrance to listen. Excited about the scavenger hunt, she saw a chance to get cash in her pocket. The beautiful woman in red basked at the attention of the men sitting around the area. However, she was cold. She needed a shawl.

Wanting to find the $1,000, she forgot about Max, the plan, and dinner. She proceeded down the corridor, searching for good hiding places for the Christmas balls. She needed that money, and her experiment to return to Max's life was not going as planned. She would give an excuse for missing dinner later.

Jill and Marty watched for Becca to enter the restaurant. The men were too busy talking about college football and didn't notice that the women were eating less.

Jill, rearranging the salt and pepper shakers, quietly asked Marty, "Where is she?"

Marty checked her cell phone and said, "I don't know. She has neither called nor texted me."

Jill responded, "How can her new plan work if she's unavailable to do her part?"

"What about the sleeping arrangement? Charlie asked me about the extra luggage in our room."

"What did you say?"

"I said we would hold Becca's luggage until she got a room."

"Good. Let's eat and enjoy this food. Everything will work out."

"I don't think I can eat. I feel yucky."

"Don't worry about Max and Becca. I got this. I'm going to have grandchildren, one way or another."

"Okay."

After a delicious meal, Max led the family to the lounge. He had no trouble exchanging the tickets one more time. They sat at table number one in the center. Max kept looking for Sarah to appear. He saved a seat just for her.

Marty left to go to the powder room and immediately texted Becca the location of the family's reserved table. Jill and Marty kept waiting for Becca to show her face. Everyone ordered drinks, but Marty, who chose water.

"Are you okay, dear?" asked Jill.

"Yes, I feel guilty about this situation. That's all," whispered Marty.

"Don't worry. Max will thank us when this is over."

Sam, from the lounge area, announced over the sound system. "Ladies and Gentlemen, please find your seats. The concert will begin in one minute."

As the fanfare began, Liz entered from the office's side door. She was running late, allowing her to avoid conversing with Jake before his concert. When Liz saw the empty chair at Max's table, she assumed Max had saved it for her.

She walked toward the front table to meet Max's guests when a gorgeous bombshell in red strolled in from the entrance and sat in the empty chair at Max's side. Liz turned around quickly and retreated to sit at the bar near Sam.

Sam asked, "Are you okay? You look as if you've seen a ghost?"

"If a ghost looks like a magazine centerfold, I have." Liz stared at the beautiful woman sitting in Max Harville's extra, reserved chair. He already had a date, a model, no doubt. Why wouldn't he? Max was a good-looking man. She couldn't compete with that woman. Liz exhaled. She thought she hated the lady in red.

She didn't have a chance to get Max now. She found it difficult to smile. The sting of rejection raised its head. She didn't need this tonight.

Max glared at Becca and then noticed his dad wasn't shocked to see her. Marty and Jill never took their eyes off the stage to avoid seeing Max's reaction to Becca joining the group. Charlie looked worried about something.

Becca said, "Thanks for allowing me to sit in this empty seat."

"How did you get in here without a ticket?"

"Are you kidding? The man at the front door was too busy looking at my dress. This is the only empty seat in the lounge. I told him my family had my ticket."

"I thought you were catching that train."

"No tickets available for the train trip. Let's enjoy the concert. I hear Jake Jones is your favorite singer now. I need to talk to you after the concert, please."

Max checked out the lounge area but did not see Sarah. He felt lucky Sarah didn't make it tonight. However, Max believed Sarah would understand the circumstances about Becca once he explained what had happened.

Max shifted his position in his seat away from Becca. Heck, he wouldn't worry about this tonight. Jake Jones was singing. He'd deal with Becca after the concert. He wished Sarah was present to enjoy the show with him. Then he remembered Sarah did not like country music. That's the reason she wasn't in the bar. Sarah's love of rock and roll had saved Max from an embarrassing situation.

Sam flipped a switch from the bar area. "Ladies and Gentlemen, The Bradford Inn is proud to introduce our guest performer tonight, Mr. Jake Jones from Nashville and Wellington."

The famous singer entered the stage, reacting to the applause and shouts from the locals. He sat on a stool and sang the lead song from his first album. Accompanied by background music, Jake controlled the sound from the stage area near the chair. As he sang, he looked across the crowd, searching for Lizzie. He found her standing by Sam at the bar. *My future bride is here. I'll make my move before she leaves.*

When Jake finished his second song, Max no longer felt anger toward Becca. He identified with the words because the singer on stage soothed his soul. The crowd yelled and clapped.

Max looked for Sarah again, hoping she would not see the woman sitting beside him. He made a mental note to write his new friend a thank you note for the tickets. He would find her tomorrow and get her phone number. When Jake began to talk, Max returned his attention to the stage.

Jake said, "I am to remind you about tomorrow's big ornament contest. How many of you are planning to participate?"

Many in the crowd raised their hands and started clapping.

Jake continued. "It sounds like fun. The annual hayride is also tomorrow beginning at 6:00 p.m. If you want to ride in the snow, be in front of the main entrance. Dress warmly and bring a blanket. You will be back in time for the seven o'clock dinner bell."

There was mumbling in the crowd.

Max's cell phone vibrated as Jake talked about his feeling about home in Wellington. He quickly answered because it was his biggest client, "Hello, Mr. Evans, hold one minute, please; I am in a crowded room."

From the stage, Jake announced, "Now, I want to invite my friend Lizzie to the stage."

Max excused himself from the table guests and headed for the entrance. He heard the crowd applauding and turned around. He smiled. His Sarah stood near the bar.

"Lizzie, come on up here," yelled Jake.

Liz exhaled, rolled her head, and slowly walked to the stage. When she reached Jake, she forced a smile.

Max stared in disbelief as he watched the scene unfold. *Jake called my Sarah the name Lizzie. Is this a joke or part of an act?* Then, he remembered his client was on the phone. Max rushed to the corridor to complete the call. Focused on the business, Max did not hear Jake onstage.

"Lizzie and I sang duets together for a while. Since I'm back in town, I hope she will join me as we sing some old tunes."

"I'm afraid I forgot those words when I transferred to business school."

Liz's former sweetheart responded, "I knew you would say that. So, I brought you a cue card with the words on it."

"I'm sure the crowd would rather hear the famous Jake Jones sing." Liz began to clap, and the audience followed her lead and led the audience to shout, "Jake, Jake, Jake."

As Liz retreated through a side stage door, Max returned to the table, thankful his client was happy. He sank in his chair, hoping Sarah would not see him sitting in the front row with the bombshell in the scanty red dress. Max pondered why his idol had hugged Sarah on the stage and called his Emerald Eyes by another name.

By the middle of the concert, Max figured out that another pretty woman had played him. His cute Sarah, who had supplied those great tickets and this reserved table, had lied to him without blinking an eye. That woman was the best actress he had ever met. No, that award goes to Becca. *I guess Sarah, no, Lizzie, plays games with men every time she rides the train. I bet she had fun entertaining me. She even continued the game in her car. Women! I'm glad I'm single.*

Max had one advantage in meeting the game player; he won Jake Jones' tickets. That cost Scary Sarah more than a few bucks.

Max vowed to enjoy the concert even though he was sitting by a liar wearing a red dress and played by a scoundrel with emerald eyes. *Forget both of them! Jake Jones and my family are the only people I trust.*

When Liz returned to the bar and approached Sam, she could barely speak. "That scene will be the talk of the town tomorrow. The locals will feel sorry for me. They will remember the famous Jake Jones dumped poor Lizzie after high school graduation."

Sam handed Liz a water bottle and told her to sit in his office. Liz walked straight to the back without looking at anyone. Sam followed in a few seconds.

Sam did not say a word to her. He sat and waited for her to control her anger. She managed the situation well but wasn't ready to hear a compliment. She wanted to punch Jake in the face. She pulled the big clip out of her hair. She shook her auburn hair until it fell around her face. She clasped her hands together, then unclasped them. She repeated this gesture several times. She stared at the floor, then the ceiling. She crossed her legs and started swinging her feet. She exhaled.

Sam spoke, "I had no idea he would pull that stunt. I promise. I will talk to Jake tonight before he leaves the lounge."

"It's not your fault. Jake said he needed to speak to me." Liz paused. "If I had met him, he would have told me about this crazy idea, and I would have said, 'No.' and not shown up tonight. So, I am partially responsible for that fiasco on stage."

"You can look at it that way, but a professional does not use a ploy like that."

Liz looked at Sam. "Thank you, Sam. I will hang in your office until the concert is over."

"Okay. I'll make sure Jake doesn't disturb you."

After the performance, Max found Sam behind the bar and thanked the bartender for the great seats and the tickets. He didn't even ask about Sarah, Lizzie, or whatever her name was. Max didn't care.

"Hey, Sam, I have a problem."

"What?"

"My ex showed up here. I need another room so she has a place to stay. I don't want to ruin Christmas for my family. Do you have a connection with the owner or someone who may find a space for me?"

"The inn is booked. There are no suites available."

"Is there a broom closet with running water? I'll stay anywhere."

Sam liked Max, and Liz did, too. "We have an apartment the owner's son occupies, and he is in France for six months on a sabbatical. Give me a second."

Sam checked with Annabelle over the phone, and she agreed to the arrangement. He instructed Max to get his luggage and meet him in the lounge in thirty minutes. Seeing fans surrounding Jake, Sam checked on Liz.

"By the way, your friend Max stopped by and said thanks for the tickets and reserved table."

"Oh, my gosh."

"What?"

"Max! He saw that whole thing. I was so mad I forgot about him being in the audience."

"I'm not following. What are you talking about?"

"He thinks I am Sarah. Now he knows I'm not."

"I will talk to him and explain."

"He will never believe my story. I had time to tell him the truth when we were off the train and in my car. Did I tell you Max hates liars?"

When Sam tried to talk to Liz, she responded, "It's too late, Sam. Don't you see? I didn't tell him my real name."

She left Sam's office by the front door and marched to her apartment. She had marked Jake off her list years ago. Now she could delete Max, too. She crawled into bed, wondering why she had such bad luck regarding men. She cried for a long time.

Later in the night, she remembered the perfect lady in red, the beauty queen. *Why was Max with a runway model if he was interested in me?* Then Liz faced reality. *Oh, he's not attracted to me! Again, I misread the signs.*

Liz rationalized she was healthy, loved her job, and was single. After an hour of tossing and turning, she recalled how sweet Max was, how funny he was, and how he loved spaghetti, too. She felt different when she was around him. It didn't matter. She lost a sweetheart of a guy all because of Jake Jones; one itsy, bitsy, little lie; and the lady in red! That woman was the answer to every man's dream. Liz's brief encounter with Max was a one-way street leading to a dead end.

Immediately after the singer took his last curtain call, the sexy lady in red walked onto the stage's apron. She placed her left hand near her diamond necklace, letting the country music star know she was single. The Harvelle family had exited the venue. When Jake approached her, Becca shook his hand and handed him a slip of paper with her phone number on it.

"Could I buy you a drink?"

"I would love that," answered Becca.

No one noticed the bellhop slip into the lounge and ask Sam to fill the last drink order for a guest before signing out for the night. While waiting, the novice detective observed the beautiful woman with Jake Jones.

She was one of those women planning something devious earlier today. The beautiful lady may be closing the deal now with the famous singer. She smiled as if she were innocent. He wished he could hear what they were saying. He needed one of those James Bond spy pens or spy flash drives on his phone to know what they were planning. *I'm sure it would be pertinent to my investigation.*

He documented the incident in his notes. **The perpetrator meets with J. Jones after the concert.** *Oh, my gosh!! Are those women going to knock off the famous country singer? This is big!*

As he turned to leave the lounge, he added a note to bring a coat and tie and leave it in his employee locker tomorrow. "CNN may interview me."

Sam said, "What did you say?"

"Oh, nothing."

The porter checked his notes and concluded that his investigation was moving faster than anticipated.

Becca was happy that Max and the family left the lounge immediately after the show. Several patrons lined up to visit Vermont's favorite son. Becca returned to the center table and waited. Some classmates introduced themselves to her and waited for Jake to join them. The singer purchased the drinks and gave his full attention to the group at the table.

"I'm Becca. I see you have many fans here."

"Yes, I grew up here in Wellington with these guys and participated in the choral program in high school. When I graduated, I headed to Nashville and got my first contract within six months."

One friend said, "You got lucky, man."

Becca said, "I can't believe you got a song produced in six months. How did you do that?"

"Lizzie, the lady I introduced tonight, and I sang as a duet in the tenth grade. I made recordings of our songs, some of which were my originals, and mailed them to several agents over the last three years in high school.

Another friend said, "That was smart of you."

"Yes, I'm glad I did. One of the agents showed interest during our senior year and scheduled a phone call. The rest is history."

Another friend asked, "We always wondered why Lizzie didn't go with you?"

"She was fine with my choice. She chose a career in business over music."

A friend responded, "I bet she regrets that now."

Jake said, "I don't know about that, but I always thought that maybe she felt she wasn't good enough to make it."

Becca commented, "Well, Lizzie made a poor decision, didn't she?"

"Yes, she's often told me how much she regretted not entering the music business. Although she doesn't sing as well as I do, my talent would have sustained her."

"Obviously, you carried her through high school," Becca reassured Jake.

The singer's friends stood to leave. After taking photos with some locals, Jake returned to the table.

"What about you? I noticed you were sitting with a group," said Jake.

"Yes, I was with my ex and his family. Now, I travel worldwide looking for the next big investment."

When Max returned to the lounge to get the key to his new living arrangements, he found Becca and his idol conversing at the reserved table.

"Excuse me, Jake. I'm Max Harvelle. I want to thank you for a great concert."

"I'm glad you came."

"Becca, you can stay in my suite tonight. Here are your keys. I will see you later."

"Thanks, I appreciate that, and we can talk. I think I will visit here for a few more minutes. Since it's late, I'll get my luggage from Marty's room tomorrow."

"Okay."

Again, Max spoke to Jake. "I hope to see another show before I leave."

"That would be great."

Becca grinned at Max and then at Jake. It was awkward for a moment. However, after Max left the lounge, Becca acted as if nothing had happened.

"Let me explain. When I arrived, there was an issue with my registration. Max is allowing me to stay in his room."

"I see." The singer didn't know precisely how to proceed. Here was a woman with money, looking for the next significant investment and staying in a room with her ex.

"We are divorced, but we are friends."

"Oh, Okay. Uh, I have not had dinner. A small restaurant on Main Street is open twenty-four hours a day. Would you be interested in eating a late meal?"

"Absolutely. It just so happens I missed dinner."

"Good. I have some ideas about a lucrative investment you might want to consider."

"I love making money. I am interested."

While Jake talked to Becca about his investment opportunities, Max entered his new place of lodging, the apartment provided by the inn's owner. The condo was typical of a man, small and quaint.

As Max unpacked his bags, he felt relieved because he had resolved the sleeping issue with Becca.

Feeling the excitement of hearing Jake Jones live, Max hummed a song from the concert. He thought about the woman he had met on the train. He was usually a good judge of character. How did he get fooled by a pretty woman named Sarah that easily? After the mess with Becca, he was more cautious of women. However, he was with Sarah for a few hours and fell for her without blinking an eye. *I don't understand this attraction that I can't forget.*

Max showered and dressed in his PJs. He couldn't quit thinking of the events of the night. First, Becca had shown up, claiming no ticket for the train ride home, and had joined his table. A country music star had exposed Sarah on the stage. He had talked about Jake Jones on the train. Sarah had never mentioned or even hinted that she knew him. However, she had purchased those tickets and arranged a head table for his family. Why would she do that?

Max considered everything he knew and remembered about Sarah. What if Sarah is her middle name? She may use that name in her business. Now that he recalled the situation, Sarah looked more agitated on that stage tonight. Heck, he didn't even know her last name.

Oh, my gosh! What if Sarah has a twin? The only way to learn the truth was to find her in the morning and get an explanation. Tomorrow Max would have all the answers. At least he had resolved the issue with Becca. Dad and Charlie won't have to deal with her.

"If my family had celebrated the holidays in Orlando, I would not be in this mess!"

His cell phone rang. "Oh my gosh. Perfect timing."

"What's up, Maxwell?"

"Margo, I can't believe you called. I spent the evening listening to my hero, Jake Jones, at a concert at my hotel."

"That country music singer will warp your mind, dude! Did you have a good time?" asked Margo Cashwell.

"Sort of."

"What happened?"

"My ex showed up at my hotel."

"You're kidding, right?"

"No."

"I can ask a police officer to contact the Wellington sheriff if you need help."

"Thanks, but I'm not worried too much about her. Why did you call?"

"I was thinking about you tonight. I'm looking for a pretty girl for your plus one for JJ and Sydnee's wedding. Do you prefer blondes?"

"I don't care about that. I want an honest woman."

"I understand. I'm working on it. Hey, send some pictures of the snow. I know Diane's kids would love to see them."

"I will do that. Anything for the Wildflowers."

When Becca arrived at suite 224 at about 2:00 a.m., she assumed Max was already asleep. She quietly took a shower and walked carefully into his room. It was dark because Max never wanted a night light. She went to the left side of the bed, always her side, and slowly pulled the soft sheet. Becca quietly dropped her damp towel on the carpet. She planned to wake Max gently.

Becca rolled to the right side to touch his back. She jumped out of bed and turned on the lights. The bed was empty. As she scanned the suite, she realized there were no suitcases, travel bags, clothes in the closet, or items in the drawers.

At first, Becca was angry. Where was he? What stunt was Max pulling? A guest must have canceled his reservation for another suite. That's the only explanation. She punched the pillows and leaned against them, reviewing her situation. Max's current behavior would not deter her; her ex was playing hard to get. That's all. Max was not over her.

Becca spoke. "Every man wants me. Look at Jake. He showed tremendous interest in me tonight."

Tomorrow, she would win the Christmas ball money and capture Max simultaneously. She had the family matron on her side. Becca snickered. Jill and Marty had fallen for that story about love and reconnecting. And if her plan with Max didn't work, Becca would turn her eyes on Jake Jones. He was making millions in the music industry.

She planned to work on all the projects, and something would stick to the wall. If she played her cards right, she'd have cash in her pocket and a ring by Christmas Day.

Becca wondered how the famous country singer felt about marriage. She laughed. *I am beautiful and can twist a man around my little finger. I now have another backup plan.*

"What if both men want to marry me? What a dilemma! I'll have to dump a man again." Becca laughed as she rearranged her pillows.

Chapter 9

When Liz awakened Saturday morning, she decided the best step to resolving the issue with Max was to call him and ask for the opportunity to explain herself. If he never spoke to her again, at least she would feel better about the situation. After all, he was a guest at the family hotel!

"Honesty is the best policy," She paused, "Although it's a little too late for that now."

She dressed in causal dark green wool slacks, a lighter green sweater, and a colorful silk scarf for the day. She rehearsed what she was going to say. She took a deep breath and called Max's room 224.

"Hello." A woman answered the phone.

Liz immediately hung up the hotel phone.

I guess Max's friend is staying in his suite. I don't have a chance to explain my situation. It's over; I'm out of here. A shopping day will help her forget the hunk with a deep voice.

As she left her apartment, she felt regret about Max. She believed they had connected, but her little lie and a supermodel had sunk the ship.

She should have told Max her real name and why she used an alias. She had opportunities to reveal the truth. Liz stretched her neck backward and sighed. *Why didn't he mention a girlfriend?*

A few minutes later, she entered the main lobby and walked upstairs to grab a coffee from the café on the mezzanine. She struggled with her thoughts.

Max couldn't believe his luck. As he entered the lobby, his Sarah walked through a side door and headed upstairs. He quietly stood directly behind her in the coffee line. Max recognized the moment Sarah realized who was now behind her.

He was delighted to find Emerald Eyes this early. Her shoulders looked tense, and she shook her head to the right, trying to relax. When she exhaled, he grinned. *Yeah, she's nervous with me behind her. Gosh, she is cute. I wonder when Whack-a-do Wanda will drop stuff and knock vases off the tables.*

When Liz smelled Max's fantastic cologne, she knew he was close. *Is he behind me?* She didn't dare look. Her face warmed. She remembered this same experience in the train dining car. She twisted the gold bracelet on her wrist and tapped her brown leather shoes. *Max may not recognize me since my hair is stacked on my head. What am I going to do? I'm next to get coffee from the attendant. Is Max too mad to talk to me, or is he ignoring me? That's all I need to embarrass myself. Max will know I'm the liar in front of him as soon as I speak.*

Max wanted to laugh when he noticed Sarah tapping her foot. *She's about to snap. I'm glad no Christmas elves are standing around.*

When the attendant asked for the order, Liz had no other alternative, and she mouthed, "I'll have coffee, no cream, and an apple Danish."

"I'm sorry; I don't understand you," said the attendant.

Liz breathed deeply and whispered the exact words, but slightly louder this time.

"I'm sorry. I can't hear what you are saying."

Of course, the server couldn't hear. Liz took a deep breath and opened her mouth to speak a little louder.

"I think Ms. Sarah wants a cup of coffee, no cream, and an apple Danish," said Max from behind Liz.

Liz turned around slowly and looked at Max, but the attendant drew her attention back to the counter.

"Here's your coffee and Danish, Miss."

When Max stepped forward and asked for apple juice and a Danish, Liz mouthed to him, "Thank you."

Max asked, "Do you have laryngitis?"

Liz mouthed, "No."

"Then what's wrong with your voice?"

Liz mouthed, "I don't have a clue. I think I'm afraid to speak."

Max leaned forward. "Open your mouth wide."

Liz followed his instructions.

"Wider."

Without thinking, Liz followed Max's orders.

Max spoke loudly. "All the parts are in there. When you exhale, air from your lungs passes past the larynx through the teeth and moves your lips. It produces sounds and words."

Max stood there and examined her extremely wide-open mouth.

Liz realized she was standing like an idiot in front of guests in line for coffee, and she knew they were staring at her with her mouth wide open. *An albatross could fly into that colossal crater in my face.* Liz closed her mouth slowly, exhaled, and rolled her head. She glanced around. Max grinned.

Liz did not look amused when she said, "I would like to speak to you privately, please."

Max exclaimed to the crowd that had gathered, "She speaks!"

The crowd applauded. Liz tried not to smile. Max grabbed Liz's elbow and guided her to a small table in the corner of the café. Max ate his Danish and waited for her to speak.

Liz was cautious as she gathered her thoughts. "Did you enjoy making fun of me?"

"I did."

She glanced at the people around her. "I believe everyone present enjoyed your fun."

Max thought for a moment. "I agree." He sipped his juice.

"Okay, I wish to apologize for telling you my name was Sarah when we met on the train."

"The lie?"

"Well, it's not really a lie."

"Your name is Sarah Lizzie?"

"No."

"Your name is Sarah Elizabeth?"

"No."

"Your name is not Sarah."

"Yes."

"You told me a lie."

"No."

Max laid his glass on the table. He was about to speak.

Liz exhaled and said, "Stop! Sarah is one of my aliases. It is a safety strategy that I use when I travel. It's what I say to protect myself against crazy men."

"So, now I am a crazy person?"

Liz struggled. She rolled her head. Every time she opened her mouth, she said the wrong words. He was making her apology difficult on purpose. Either Max was punishing or teasing her; she did not know which.

Liz blurted out, "Why aren't you having breakfast with your date?" *On my gosh, why did I say that? This man is driving me crazy!*

"Who?"

"I assume the bombshell in red from last night?" *I have lost control of my mouth! What is happening to me?*

"I don't know where she is. Forget her. Tell me about this safety strategy thing that makes you lie."

"I didn't lie!"

"Your name is Sarah?"

"No."

Max looked at her, waiting.

"Okay, I told a little lie." Liz gave up.

Max grinned, "I win."

Liz threw her hands up and exhaled.

Max quickly looked around, making big gestures.

"Max? What are you doing?"

"I'm looking for a Christmas elf for you to knock over."

Liz looked away, trying not to laugh.

Max loved sparring with her. She was competitive and didn't like losing. She was cute even when she was frustrated and knocking down decorations.

Liz explained why she had created that habit when she traveled for business. After a lengthy explanation, she stopped talking to drink her coffee. It was cold.

Max called a server and ordered Liz another cup of hot coffee.

He is a real gentleman. It's a shame he reunited with his ex. What am I doing talking to him, anyway? "I called your suite this morning to apologize, but a female answered."

"You did? Oh, you called room 224?"

"That's your suite. That's where I sent your notes!"

"That was my ex. Becca is staying in my suite. The inn allowed me to stay in someone's apartment to escape her. Wasn't that nice of the owner?"

Liz didn't believe him at first. "Yes, how did you arrange that?"

"The bartender in the lounge negotiated with the hotel."

"Interesting. Since I have apologized for my name, I guess I need to go. I've taken enough of your time. Do you truly accept my apology?"

"Yeah."

"And you are not back with your ex?" *Why did I bring that woman up again? I sound like a jealous female. I wonder what he is thinking of me now.*

"I had no idea Becca was coming here. She's probably leaving today. Like I said, forget her. Do I call you Liz or Lizzie?"

"Liz. I gave up Lizzie when I became a college student."

"What about Jake Jones?"

"What about him?"

"When did you sing with him?"

"Jake and I sang as a duet in high school. We earned scholarships in music. But after high school graduation, he chose to go to Nashville. I changed to business school. Last night was the first time I have talked to him since he left town years ago."

"But why didn't you tell me you knew him when I said he was my favorite singer?"

"It wasn't a friendly break-up, and I told you I don't like country music."

Max found Liz endearing. They talked about the inn, and Max remarked about the renovations, the concert last night, and his family's enjoyable stay there.

"I'm glad I ran into you this morning. I feel better now that we have all the little inconsistencies settled," remarked Liz.

"Me, too."

"Well, I'll get going." Liz stood to leave.

"Wait."

“Okay,” Liz returned to her chair.

“Since we’ve had three conversations, and I believe I have proven I am not a crazy man, may I have your phone number? Maybe we could go out or something when you have time this week.”

Liz looked at Max, pulled a small notepad out of her purse, and wrote her number. When Liz began to stand, Max walked around and helped her with her chair.

“Liz?”

She looked up. Max placed his hand under her chin and gently kissed her. *What the heck made me do that? She’ll think I am crazy!*

Liz cleared her throat. “That was nice!”

“I thought so, too.” Max gently looked at Liz. “Normally, I don’t kiss women this early in a relationship. However, in Madison County, when a lady gives a man her phone number, it gives the man permission to kiss her.”

Not believing a word he said, Liz reacted, “That’s a friendly community where you live!”

“Yeah, it is.”

They stood looking at each other.

Max said, “I’ll call you.”

“Okay.”

“Later,” said Max.

“Okay.”

“Today.”

“I look forward to it.”

“I will call.”

“I believe you. Remember, it’s Liz, not Sarah.

“I won’t forget that.”

“Good. Bye.” Liz left the area to go shopping. She wasn’t sure her feet were touching the ground.

Max stayed in the café, thinking about his breakfast with Liz. He had lost his ability to think around that girl. His instincts were correct. She was a sweetheart of a girl and nothing like Becca. *I can’t believe I kissed her. What was I thinking? But it felt good.* Max finished his juice. *And Liz and I have no more secrets between us.*

Chapter 10

A few minutes later, guests, primarily young people, gathered in the lobby, ready to begin the Christmas scavenger hunt. Becca, dressed in a gray warmup suit, arrived last. Frustrated at her position in the crowd, she pushed her way to the center. She wanted an advantageous location to begin.

At precisely 9 a.m., all the participants joined the countdown when Annabelle shouted. "10,9,8,7,6,5,4,3,2,1. The Christmas Scavenger contest begins. Good luck to everyone."

Participants moved fast, looking for the ornaments. Becca shoved the children out of her way. The bellhop darted in and out of the crowd, hoping to hear the name Sarah mentioned. At one point, Becca slammed him into the wall. Taller guests checked in the Christmas tree while others peeked under furniture and in vases. Laughter and shouts of excitement filled the main corridor as the holiday music played in the background.

Becca began with the Christmas decorations on a small table in the corridor. A young married couple examined the dazzling decorations on the gifts under the white Christmas tree at the entrance to the lobby. Soon, a little girl yelled and then giggled with laughter when she found ornament #2 in a giant red and green flowerpot filled with white poinsettias in the corridor leading to the restaurant.

"I found it in the white plant outside the ladies' bathroom in the hallway."

People congratulated the happy child as she passed through the crowd. Everyone encouraged the child but Becca, who cringed. That spot was on her list to check later. Becca watched with hatred as the youngster carried the ornament in her tiny hands. Becca wanted to snatch it from the obnoxious brat when the winner handed the adorable ball to the clerk at the registration desk.

Like clockwork, the photographer arrived to take the souvenir picture. An elf ran into the lobby, hugged the winner, and handed her a big check for $500. The little girl's proud parents embraced her.

Contestants gathered around, clapping their hands, and congratulated the first winner.

The bells played "I Wish you a Merry Christmas," signaling someone had found an ornament. Contestants sang along; everyone except Becca. She left the momentous occasion to get a head start on the contest.

Annabelle shouted, "One down and two left."

The contestants exited the lobby, searching for the two remaining Christmas decorations. Becca was a fierce competitor and unhappy she lost the first $500. She reviewed her list and sneaked in the opposite direction of those stupid people.

Marty and Jill, dressed in Christmas sweaters and white wool slacks, exited elevator #1 and walked into a large group of people. Marty followed her mother to the corridor, where a short wooden bench stood near a bay window. The view of the white snow-covered grounds was spectacular. An antique wooden coffee cart situated along a wall provided coffee for guests. After each got coffee, they sat on the light gray cushioned bench.

Jill spoke first. "I'm dying to know. Did Becca stay in your suite?"

"No," Marty gasped. "But she called this morning and asked Charlie to take her suitcase to Max's room. Our plan is succeeding." They saluted their coffee cups in celebration.

Becca, her clothes showing dust and dirt, ran by, looking everywhere and checking her list. Marty and Mom watched as she passed them. Becca was engrossed in the contest and didn't even notice Jill or Marty.

Jill called, "Becca!"

Becca stopped and glanced toward her former in-laws. She did not have time for those people. She was on a new mission now, but she moved toward them.

Jill offered her coffee, which Becca hastily declined. "How was last night, dear?"

Becca assumed Jill was discussing the concert and answered, "It was fabulous. I slept like a baby when I finally got to sleep. I would love to discuss it, but I am focused on the contest. It's so much fun. We'll talk later." Becca fled to continue the scavenger hunt.

"Mother, do you know what this means? We have done it. I think I am going to cry. Max must be so happy." Marty hugged her mom.

The bellhop walked near them and stopped. He observed the two women who were crying and hugging each other. Maybe these ladies had second thoughts or were too deep in their sinister plan, or a significant problem existed. Perhaps they suffered from abuse or had lost all their money. He felt sad for them. They needed counseling.

In his investigation book, he wrote that a gang of two was crying and may have second thoughts. He moved away before the ladies noticed him.

"Sweetheart, it's a Christmas miracle. I told Max something good would happen."

They sipped their coffee and marveled at what they had accomplished. The ladies congratulated each other on their wise planning.

Jill stopped to focus. "We have a wedding to plan."

"Mother, this is exciting. They should renew their vows here just as they did five years ago."

"I agree. I will talk to Ms. Annabelle and see if we can schedule that quaint little chapel for the ceremony. You check at the front desk and see if the inn has a notary who can perform the ceremony."

Hearing a shout near the main restaurant, all the contestants herded past the lobby toward the restaurant. The bellhop hurried behind the loud group taking notes. An elderly gentleman walking with a cane met the participants in the corridor. He held a $500 Christmas fixture marked #1 in his shaking hand. The group clapped and congratulated him as they followed the second winner to the lobby.

The elf and photographer entered and took pictures. Everyone rejoiced except Becca. She looked frantic now. The Christmas bells rang again. The participants sang, "We Wish You a Merry Christmas!"

After the brief celebration, everyone scattered. Becca rushed outside to check the front of the inn. Someone probably hid something out here. The inquisitive bellhop noticed her strange behavior and decided to follow her. However, he stopped when he heard an interesting conversation from the coffee station nearby.

"We have to go shopping for new clothes."

"You're right! We must be careful with our money. Oh, and we should ask that photographer to take the pictures."

"Yes, we want proof this thing happened."

The bellhop immediately recognized the hideous criminals and hid behind a column. He opened his notebook. With shaking hands, he wrote. **The ladies had their clothes destroyed. They hired the inn photographer to take the pictures as proof of the "thing." Watching their $$.** They may sue for millions of dollars. Whatever the "thing" was, it was big. Since the two women were crying earlier, they probably plan to sue for emotional damages and financial support. The proud bellhop felt his studies in criminology were a positive factor in helping the investigators on this case. He would serve as the key witness. His documentation would send these vicious criminals to the electric chair.

"I need more information before I report my findings. I must keep all my notes. I might author a best seller, and then Gayle King might ask for an interview. Oprah might select my work for her Book of the Month Club. The possibilities are endless. I'm about to be famous." He paused when he overheard the ladies' new plan.

Jill and Marty considered their tasks. Then Marty said, "Hey, I have a great idea."

"What?"

"Let's get Jake Jones in on this! Max would love that, but we will keep it a secret from Max until the end."

"I don't know. That would cost a ransom, and you know who would die!"

"You're right; he would."

"But it's an option to consider. I don't think the guy will do it, but I will ask him. We must get the job done. Let's grab our coats. It's cold outside."

As the women left the area, the bellhop shook in fear as he scribbled what he had heard. Beads of sweat formed on his brow. **Somebody will kidnap someone. Jake Jones is an accomplice. There is a ransom. Someone may die!** Is Max the victim? These women were pure evil. They look so innocent; no one would expect them to be horrible criminals. Could the missing Sarah be a part of this evil scheme? What about the beautiful lady? Where does she fit into this dastardly deed? Poor Max won't know about it until it's all over! "Oh, this is bigger than big!"

The bellhop wanted to report this to the authorities immediately. The inn's reputation was at stake, and someone might die.

When he phoned the hotel's security center, he discovered a substitute was in the office. This new guy might be a plant. It happened all the time in the movies. The new man in uniform might be the "godfather."

The bellhop whispered. "I don't know whom to trust. I will collect enough evidence that Perry Mason couldn't save these conniving, wicked women. I was born for this assignment."

Chapter 11

Later, Saturday morning, Jake exited elevator #1 and headed to the lounge to rehearse and to check the sound system for tonight's concert, and he hoped to catch Lizzie. He needed to see her today. He had screwed up when he had asked her to come on the stage last night. His plan took a hit as a result. He would apologize today and begin again. He had saved the new song he had written for her.

Max stood at the bottom of the mezzanine steps, entering Liz's phone number in his cell phone contact list. Not looking, he walked down the steps and into the pathway of Jake Jones, bumping into him.

"Sorry, man… I was…

"Oh, it's great to see you again, Max."

"I enjoyed your concert."

The singer and Max chatted about the music. Then, Jake thought about the sleeping arrangements for Becca, and he was more than a little curious. "Max, did you get the room arrangements for you and Becca resolved?"

Max had forgotten about Becca but said, "Oh, yeah. There was plenty of room in my suite for her."

"Good."

Max continued, referring to the concert. "Man, I had a great time last night."

"Really?"

Max reminisced, “Yeah. In fact, it may have been the best night of my life.”

Jake asked, “Uh, it was that good?”

“Yeah, it was!”

Since the performer had to practice, he excused himself and headed down the corridor. He shook his head and thought Max and Becca had a unique relationship. They were divorced but together for the holidays. Jake reached into his pocket to retrieve the note from Becca. It listed her phone number.

Jake paused. “I wonder how much money this woman has.”

The busy bellhop rushed by at that moment with a message for Annabelle. He stopped when he heard Jake talking to himself. Oh, Jake was taking the bait. Criminal activity had been progressing quickly since the godfather entered the picture.

He immediately added the latest information to his notebook. The bellhop re-read his list of details for clarity and headed to the security office. Could the beautiful woman be the missing Sarah? It was time to file his report with the top guy if the chief was back in the office. The pieces were beginning to fit together. The bellhop wondered if he would get a promotion or a monetary reward for his excellent detective work.

Ignoring the strange behavior of the bellhop, Jake walked to the coffee station and poured himself a cup. Walking toward the lounge, he reflected on his proposal plan and how it worked. He needed to get to Lizzie. Since he practiced early this morning, he hoped she might stop by the lounge to see Sam.

He placed Becca’s note in his pocket. He would add her name to his list of possible investors. Jake thought about his cash flow. Since he was performing at home, his suite was compliments of the inn. Step two was to reconnect with his former sweetheart. Jake’s goal was to find her, tell her he loved her, and apologize for his colossal mistake. During one of his concerts, he planned to sing a new song just for Lizzie.

He would kneel on one knee and propose to his high school sweetheart on stage. That proposal would make headlines in the news. Great publicity. Heck! He forgot to call the radio station and his agent to have reporters at the lounge. Now, he had to postpone the song's debut until another night. He’d dedicate an old song to Lizzie tonight.

He turned around to go to the main desk and leave Annabelle a note. He needed Lizzie's phone number. Now that the inn was in its third year, Jake figured it was making a good profit. He had heard Lizzie had an advantageous position in the company with a big salary.

They would get married quickly at the inn, and he would resurrect his career as a country music star. Lizzie would cover his expenses until he got back on his feet and got the new album going.

He thought about Becca. Now that's a beautiful woman. She has all the right stuff in all the right places and displays it to the world. She has money to burn. Jake didn't want to marry her, just her cash. Becca was the type who would insist on traveling with him everywhere.

Now, Lizzie had money, but she wouldn't fly. Jake and Lizzie were more compatible!

When Jake entered the lounge, he asked Sam for Lizzie's location. Sam claimed he had not seen her today.

"Look, I need to talk to Lizzie. Just give me her phone number."

"After that stunt you pulled last night, she doesn't want to speak to you."

"I tell you what, you call her on your phone, and I will talk to her."

"Jake, her phone is turned off this morning. I tried to reach her earlier."

"I see you are still Lizzie's big protector."

"That's right." Sam refused to be Jake's ally.

Jake moved toward the stage to practice. As he strummed the guitar, he wondered if Annabelle would provide Lizzic's phone number. Somebody had her number, and he was going to get it. *I must marry Lizzie before this year is over.*

Max remembered that the hayride would occur tonight. *I think I'll invite Liz to go on a date.* Thinking Liz would enjoy the event, he searched everywhere for her. She did not respond to his texts or phone calls. By this time, Max needed more than juice and a Danish. Walking toward the lobby among the scavenger hunt participants, he noticed everyone laughing and having fun. *What a great Christmas activity!*

He stopped when his dad invited Charlie and him for brunch at the Snak Shack housed in the next building. Max accepted and texted Liz, extending an invitation to the hayride one more time.

When Max noticed Becca heading his way, he carefully stepped out of her view behind a large leafy green plant. He glanced at his phone. If Liz agreed to go with him on the hayride, he would know where he stood with her.

He almost didn't recognize his ex. Becca looked terrible. She wore a sloppy warm-up suit. The top showed streaks of dirt. Her hair fell in strands from her ponytail held with a colored clip. She wore no make-up. She must have lost something. She was looking everywhere. *Ahhhh! She's one of the scavengers.*

Max observed her for a minute. *Why is she participating in the scavenger hunt? That's not her style. Does she need money? That may be why she didn't catch the train home. She's broke.* After she passed, he quietly headed for the front door.

When Max entered the Snak Shack, his dad waved his hand. Dan was the president of Orange County Bank, and Charlie was one of its investment brokers. Everyone ordered their food and talked about the bank and football. It didn't take them long to mention the name of Becca, which provided the perfect time for Max to get answers about the Christmas trip.

"Did either of you know Becca was going to be here this Christmas?" asked Max.

"I didn't, did you, Charlie?" asked Dad.

"No," responded Charlie.

Max didn't dare mention he thought Mom and Marty knew and were part of the scheme.

"Why did you want to come back here for Christmas?" Dad asked.

"I didn't." Max said, "I begged Mom to change the destination."

Dad glanced at Charlie, who exclaimed it certainly wasn't his idea. They both sat there drinking their coffee. Max just let them ponder the situation.

After the meal, Dad asked, "So where is Becca staying?"

"In my suite."

Dad peeked at Charlie. "Interesting."

At that time, Max knew if he said he stayed in an apartment behind the inn, Becca would find him. Mom and Marty would never keep that fact a secret. Therefore, he let the men think whatever their minds wanted to create.

"Did you sleep well?" asked Charlie.

"Yep, had a great night."

Dad winked at Charlie. Max didn't see the reaction because his phone rang. Liz was calling.

"Hey, I tried to reach you after breakfast," said Max.

"Yes, I just returned to my suite, checked my phone, and read your messages. I did not take my phone today. When I shop, I like to enjoy the experience and have no hassles."

"I understand."

"I would love to go on the hayride tonight," Liz said.

"You would?"

"Yes, I'll meet you at the main entrance at about 5:50 p.m. I'll bring a blanket."

"Okay, uh, one question."

"What?"

"Do they allow any PDA on this hayride?"

"What is PDA?"

"Public Display of Affection."

Liz laughed. "Oh, I heard Vermont had adopted a Madison County custom."

"Well then, expect a kiss. That's one of my best features."

Liz remembered his first kiss and said, "I know."

Max was beaming like a schoolboy. "See you tonight."

Max took a sip of his tea and could not quit smiling. He momentarily forgot he sat with his father and brother-in-law at the table. He glanced at his family, gawking at him when he remembered they were present.

"What?"

"Son, you sound like a teenager with a high school crush," Dad shared.

"It's different this time."

"How?" asked Charlie.

"She's wonderful. She listens to me when we talk. I can't stop thinking about her."

"Son, I'm a little surprised to hear this, but I'm happy for you."

"To be honest, I'm shocked myself."

"This news is going to make my wife very happy."

"I think I will go shopping for a Christmas gift."

When Max reached into his pocket for cash to pay his bill, Dad said. "I got this."

"Thanks. See you tonight at 7:30."

Max rushed out and ran into his mom and sister in front of the building. He informed them that their husbands were in the sandwich shop. He paused to take snow photos and texted them to Diane Harris. Margo had requested it for Diane's children.

Before Max entered the jewelry store, Diane called, "Thank you for the snow photos. The kids are not home right now, but they will love them. How is it going up there?"

"I'm having a great time. I met someone on the train coming up."

"You did not share this earlier. Wait a minute. The girls will kill me if I don't include them in this call. Hang on."

"Sydnee, are you there?" asked Diane.

"Yes, and Margo is with me. What's up?"

"Max has met someone special."

The Wildflowers asked twenty questions, which Max gladly answered. They agreed to get together when his special friend visited Madison County.

Jill and Marty stood on the street watching Max laugh as he talked on the phone and then entered the store. Jill high-fived her daughter. Approaching the cafe, the ladies agreed to tell Dan and Charlie about the wedding plans. They managed to carry all their purchases to the table without disturbing many people.

After Jill and Marty had ordered their lunch, Dan announced new facts about Max. "He's in love again."

Marty and Jill shrieked loudly. They started clapping and hugging each other.

"We know," shared Marty.

"We just went shopping for wedding clothes," said Jill. "Tell us what you know."

"First, did you initiate this whole situation with Becca?" asked Dan.

Jill looked at her husband. "We knew Becca was coming here, and she suggested the family return for the holidays."

"It worked this time, but don't do this again, Honey. Max can make his own decisions."

Dan and Charlie told them everything that had transpired, from the phone call to the giddy Max. The girls then shared what they knew. When their tea arrived, the four made a toast to the happy couple.

Dan ended the toast. "Repeat!"

"I see grandchildren in our future," exclaimed Jill.

All agreed, and the girls shared their plans for the pending nuptials. A scream and the sounds of a bell ringing stopped the conversation. The scavenger hunt was over, and activity in the hallways would calm down.

A crowd passed in front of the café and headed to the inn's lobby. Somebody had found the $1,000 Christmas ornament. The patrons in the sandwich shop clapped their hands.

At the end of the group, Becca dragged behind. She looked like a vagrant. The hair that had been in a ponytail was now falling down her back. Her clothes were dirty and torn in several places. She had been in dirt and grass, looking for the last ball. She was hobbling because her shoe had formed a blister on her foot.

As the group stared at Becca when she rambled near the Snak Shack, Dan said, "Honey, we must be careful."

Jill and the rest of the group looked at Dan.

"If Max sees Becca looking like that, he may not marry her. Or maybe love is blind."

They all agreed and roared laughing.

"Jill, you and Marty must try the Christmas red velvet cake. It is delicious."

"We will."

Dan hesitantly inquired, "Wife, how much will this repeat wedding cost me?"

Jill responded, "Let's just say. It won't kill you."

Chapter 12

Becca returned to Max's suite, exhausted from the hideous holiday activity. She had searched everywhere and had not found one ornament. She was disgusted. What a stupid game! She was filthy and sweaty. She wanted to soak for at least an hour to get all the grime off. She deserved a massage for all the work she had done today.

She wondered where her ex-husband was. She had looked for him while she scouted for ornaments. She hoped Jill and Marty worked on the plan. If events didn't improve soon, she would be forced to call her mom and borrow money to fly home. Becca tried to call Max, but he didn't answer. *Where is he?*

While Becca recovered from the scavenger hunt, Liz returned to her apartment to work for a few hours. First, she checked with Sam to ask if there were any business issues, and second, if he knew the whereabouts of Jake Jones.

As she looked at her computer, thoughts of Max resurfaced. Is the hayride a date? That idea made her happy. She needed to tell somebody.

"Hey, Sam!"

"This is the second call in five minutes. What's up?"

"Are you busy?"

"I'm swamped with work, but I'm never too busy for you."

"Thanks. You are so good to me."

"I know."

"I'm calling because I won't be attending the concert tonight, nor will I go to the lounge for any reason."

"I wasn't expecting you to come!"

"I have a good reason for skipping those events."

"Should I sit down for this information?"

"Quit teasing me, Sam. I have a serious situation."

"Okay, I'm ready."

"An acquaintance asked me to go on the hayride."

"Well, when you bribe someone with $180 worth of tickets, he may take you out on a date."

"Sam!" Liz jumped out of her chair.

"Have you noticed you call me Sam louder when you are perturbed with me?"

"That is not accurate. I never raise my voice. I speak with conviction."

"I see."

Liz returned to her seat and thought about Sam's comment.

"Liz, are you still there?"

"You think he feels obligated to invite me because I bought those tickets for him?" Liz chewed on a fingernail.

"Liz, he's a nice guy. If he asked you out on a date, he wanted to be with you. It has nothing to do with tickets. Are you chewing a fingernail right now?"

Liz immediately removed her fingernail from her mouth. "No. But what if he asked me as a thank you for the tickets?"

"Go on the hayride. You will have your answer. Have fun. Um, Liz.?"

"Yes?"

"Are you going on the 6 o'clock hayride?"

"Yes. Why?"

"You remember how to act on a date, don't you? Do I need to give you a few pointers? It's been a long time."

"Sam!"

"I love the way you speak with conviction! See you tomorrow, Sweetheart."

Sam loved teasing Liz. Unfortunately, he did not realize Jake had stopped playing the guitar and had heard every word the bartender had said.

Later in the afternoon, Becca's phone rang. She thought it might be Max trying to reach her. "Hello?"

"Becca, this is Jake Jones!"

"Oh, hi."

"Have you made any plans for 6:00 p.m. today?"

"I just happen to be free at that time."

"Meet me in front of the lobby at about 5:45 p.m. Let's go on a hayride! Bring a blanket."

"That sounds like a grand idea. I would love to go. See you then. Thanks."

Tonight, Jake planned to take his guitar on the hayride and give a private concert to the guests. No charge. His fans would love it. He would see Lizzie's date and get an opportunity to talk to her. He had a few more days to solve his problem. He must share his feelings for her and ask for forgiveness. Then he would propose. If he failed, the implementation of plan B with Becca would follow. Jake didn't know who the date was, but he wasn't worried. He was positive he'd win her back.

Jake grabbed a pencil. A love song was forming in his mind. Jake quickly wrote the lyrics of his next great hit. "For The Love of Lizzie." He paused when he finished writing the lyrics. When Lizzie heard this song, she'd realize he was sorry for his mistakes and would want to be with him forever.

He laughed. "If Lizzie misses the hayride, I'll change the words to Becca. I'm a dang genius."

While Jake Jones practiced and wrote songs in the lounge, guests and inn staff prepared for the hayride. The bellhop reported his information about the missing Sarah to the clerk at the main desk.

"Have you found Sarah?" the clerk asked, tapping his pen on the counter.

"No, Sir, and I have looked everywhere."

"I've been thinking," the clerk said.

"What have you been thinking?"

"Sarah might be a code name."

"Code?" The young porter thought about that idea, and then his face turned red, and sweat formed on his brow.

"Boy, are you alright? Should I call the paramedic?"

"No, I have another problem, Sir."

The future FBI agent rushed from the room. He sat and scribbled in his notebook when he found a blank space. **S A R A H**. He wrote words and scratched them out. The boy stressed over the idea. After a few minutes, the bellhop laid his pen down and looked for hidden cameras. He placed his hands over the notebook so no eyes could see what he had discovered. **Secure the Assassination of Rogue Agent at Hotel.**

With a quivering voice, the bellhop whispered, "I have stumbled on an international plot. There's a double agent in our midst. I know too much. My life may be in danger."

When the nervous bellhop returned to the front desk, the clerk urged him to keep working on the task and to watch the Max guy.

When the briefing concluded, the bellman said, "I guess Mr. Max stays in his room most of the time. I think I will stay on the second floor and watch suite 224. Maybe he will lead me to the MPA."

"What is MPA?"

"Missing Person in Action, Sir."

"Did you learn that acronym in your criminology class?"

"No, Sir, I invented it."

"You invented it?"

"You know. Made it up."

The clerk shook his head. "Have you ever heard of MBA, young man?"

"All I know is Major Basketball Association and Major Baseball Association. What else does it stand for?"

"Missing Brain in Action."

"Ha, ha, that's funny, Sir!"

If the clerk knew what I knew, he would be amazed. My brain is about to make history! I'm the new Bond, James Bond, and I must watch my back!

Chapter 13

When the beautiful lady in red and white stepped out of Max's suite, the bellhop stood nearby on official duty. *That's odd. It's too early for dinner. Maybe she is going on the hayride.* The bellhop greeted her and deduced he needed to get on that hayride. The bellhop joined the alleged criminal on the elevator.

When they arrived on the first floor, the bellhop ran to get his jacket. He left the building through a side door and jumped onto the trailer. He chose to sit on the southwest corner near the tractor to observe everything. Unfortunately, two robust men and their hefty wives, carrying huge plaid blankets, wobbled onto the trailer and chose the hay bales in front of the bellhop, blocking his view. This seating arrangement forced the bellhop to teeter on the edge of the trailer.

The bellhop was stuck and could not change his position. At least he was on the trailer. Behind those guys might be better, anyway. He was invisible. He would crawl over those people if he had to take a bullet for someone.

Becca made her grand entrance in the lobby at 5:55 p.m. She arrived early to pose gracefully in front of a column near the main entrance. During the scavenger hunt, she had noticed the white in the wood would make her red outfit pop. Everyone going on the tacky hayride would envy her in that stunning outfit. She opened the massive doors and walked onto the front porch. She leaned against the pillar as if posing for a couture magazine.

She waited. After a few moments, chill bumps popped up on her arms. She forgot how cold it was outside. She had been hot all day, running, climbing, searching under chairs and tables, and looking into dirty flowerpots. She rubbed her arms to keep warm. *What is it with this air in Vermont? My nose is dripping, and I have no handkerchief. I never need tissues. I'm shaking, for goodness sake. Will someone please stop the yucky snow for a little while?*

As Becca stood on the porch shivering, she remembered that Jill and Marty, along with their spouses, might go on the hayride at this hour. If they saw her with Jake, someone might destroy her plan for financial freedom. What if Max was with them? She concluded she needed to get out of the frigid weather for more than one reason.

Becca was freezing and wanted her mink coat to protect her from the horrendous arctic temperature. The hayride had been a bad idea, and she needed to exit the area quickly. She would apologize to Jake later.

As Becca cautiously manipulated her legs to avoid slipping, the little brat who won the first ornament in the scavenger hunt earlier in the day completed building her beautiful snowman at the bottom of the steps. The child rushed to enter the building. As she approached the steps near the column where Becca huddled, shivering, the little girl slipped as she landed on the last step and slid feet first into Becca's long legs.

Becca did not see the child because she was staring at the front door. She lost her balance, shrieking loudly. The lady in red tumbled backward with her arms flying in the air and fell into a pile of snow blown from the sidewalk.

Guests walking out of the inn watched in shock as the little girl tried several times to stand up but kept slipping down. The clerk at the front desk heard the commotion and ran to the porch. When he stepped on the wet section of the porch, he slid and landed on the woman struggling in the snow.

"Get off me! Move, you moron!"

"Ma'am, I am trying, but the snow is slippery."

"Remove yourself from my body. Now!"

Someone helped the clerk stand while another man pulled Becca to her feet. When she regained her balance, she resembled a wet mummy. The snow-covered victim glared at the little pest, who giggled at the situation.

Dirty, gray snow and dark, runny mud drizzled over Becca's beautiful red outfit. Her wet hair dripped on her elegant sweater and fell over her face. Her mascara formed black circles with tears around her eyes.

"I am freezing! Get out of my way this minute. All of you! Open that door so that I can get inside!"

A small crowd formed around the accident when Becca screamed and commanded someone to help her. Some guests saw an opportunity to jump on the hayride quickly and grab a seat. On the trailer, both prominent men who sat in front of the bellhop stood to see what the fuss was about. Their actions pushed the bellhop back, causing him to lose his balance.

The bellhop attempted to correct his stance as his arms danced in the air, but he flopped off the trailer, landing on a pile of soft snow. Thank goodness the fall didn't kill him.

A paramedic was on duty for each ride. However, he was at the back of the vehicle. He was busy helping people get onto the trailer. He ran to assist the desk clerk with the screaming lady and was unaware the bellhop floundered on the other side.

Entering the lobby, Becca ordered the paramedic to take his hands off her body. She gracefully shuffled as best she could to the elevator. The glamorous lady never looked at the crowd gathering to see the commotion. She felt the gazes and heard snickers from guests staring at her.

A trail of water, snow, and mud followed Becca. She looked like a waif gliding across the beautiful marble floor. Her appearance reminded everyone of The Ghost of Christmas Past. She failed to ask about the health of the desk clerk or that brat child who had ruined her evening and gorgeous outfit.

Jake couldn't reach the entrance to the lobby because a huge crowd stood in the way. He couldn't see what was happening, and finally, the group scattered enough to see the housekeeping staff mopping the floor. Annabelle supervised quietly and talked with guests.

With the front entrance temporarily locked, Jake exited through a side door. He quickly secured a seat at the trailer's northwest corner and saved it for Becca.

People carrying blankets climbed onto the vehicle, grabbing a place to sit. Sometimes the tractor was more exciting for kids than the actual ride. The trailer had benches secured for senior citizens and hay bales for the younger folks. The trailer accommodated about sixty people at one time.

Max and Liz were among the last couples to join the group and grabbed the last two seats near the rear. Light snow fell as if on cue as the trailer pulled away from the curb. Adults said, “Ahhh,” and laughed and began putting on their hats. No one noticed the bellhop stranded, digging himself out of the snow.

Jake looked so hard for Lizzie to climb aboard that he forgot about his date. With everyone wearing hats and oversized coats, he could not distinguish her from anyone else. Then he remembered Becca. *Where is Becca? Lizzie is not on the trailer, either. I’m stuck here for an hour. My plan for the evening is wrecked.*

Jake was about to disembark and return to the hotel when he saw Lizzie sitting on the southeast corner stack of hay. He gritted his teeth when Max put his arm around Lizzie. Jake didn’t like what he saw. *What is she doing with that Max guy? He’s with Becca, and now he’s with Lizzie? He’s a creep. It’s a good idea my date didn’t show because Lizzie would get highly jealous when she saw me with Becca. I must act smarter. I will approach my old sweetheart after the hayride.*

When Jake Jones announced he was providing the entertainment tonight, Liz tensed. Max felt her body react and misunderstood her body’s response.

“You don’t like country music, do you?” Max asked.

“No, but I will listen to it because I know you do.”

Then, Jake sang a popular song, "Please Forgive Me, Sweetheart.”

“I know a way to tune country music out of your mind,” said Max.

“Did you bring earplugs?”

“No.”

“That’s the only way.”

“No, there’s another way.”

Max kissed Liz. “Did that help you forget Jake Jones?”

“Who?”

Liz took Max’s hand and held it. She relaxed beside him and enjoyed the hayride, soft snow flurries, and the twinkling of the Christmas lights decorating the street.

Max noticed the clouds clearing. "Liz, look at the sky."

Liz observed the bright stars. Others near them gazed at the heavens, too. A shooting star streaked across the dark sky. Everyone yelled and started clapping, interrupting Jake's private concert.

"Wow, the city of Wellington knows how to control the stars. I wish my parents could see this display."

"Max, text them and recommend they go on the hayride. They must be at the front of the inn at the beginning of the hour. The trip is too beautiful to miss."

"You're right."

Since no one was listening to his music, Jake stopped singing to join the others, impressed by the beauty of the night. The tractor slowed, and another falling star streaked across the sky. The audience reacted in jubilation.

Most guests did not want to depart when the trailer returned to the inn. The hayride was a tremendous success. One rider questioned how the inn paid for the falling star show. Other guests asked also. Max leaned down and kissed Liz again as the riders talked among themselves. She kissed him back, totally forgetting Jake Jones.

"Would you like to go for a carriage ride? We could stop downtown and eat dinner."

"Sure. Since we have these blankets, it would be a suitable time to tour Wellington."

"I'll go secure a carriage. Stay here."

"Okay."

While Max arranged the carriage ride, Liz folded the blankets. When she had completed the task, Jake was standing by her.

"Lizzie, I know you have been busy, but I want to meet you tomorrow. We need to talk." Jake glanced toward Max.

Liz looked at Jake. "I don't have time. Share all of your issues with Sam."

"Jake," Max said when he returned. "I didn't know you were providing a mini-concert tonight on the hayride."

"It helped my warm-up for the show tonight. With that said, I'll head to the lounge. See you."

"Yeah." Max assisted Liz as she stepped onto the carriage. "I'm glad we chose the first ride."

"Me, too."

While the carriage strolled through town, Max teased, "I think tonight, I will educate you on the attributes of loving country music."

Liz pretended to exit the chariot. Max grabbed her and put the blankets around her.

"I've changed my mind about that," said Max.

"Good."

Max put his arm around her. "This will prevent you from jumping out of the carriage if I say something else you disagree with."

"You think one arm will stop me?"

Max moved his right hand to grab her hands. "No, but two will."

Max and Liz observed the twinkling lights as the horse clopped down Main Street.

Max said, "Seeing the lights at night is spectacular."

"I suggest we stop here at this diner at the end of the ride. It serves great food and fabulous hot chocolate. Carolers are performing in thirty minutes."

"I like that idea."

"When Wellington was a small town, the leaders met to discuss the community's growth. They planned the streets and the parks. Women showed up to give advice and suggested the village become a venue for weddings and other celebrations. That meeting is what started Wellington as it is today."

"Interesting."

"Did you know all the stores on Main Street are designated by vendor type? If a business owner sells his store, only that type of commerce can buy it. Like a flower shop."

"Can the town legally do that?"

"I don't know, but that's a rule. The leaders bought real estate across from the central park for future development back in the fifties. Today, one is a parking lot, and the rest provide the space for a small arena for outdoor concerts."

"That's why everything is so perfect. How do you know so much about Wellington?"

"You didn't read the chamber of commerce brochure sent in The Bradford Inn packet, did you?"

"I remember you said that, but I forgot to ask Mother about it."

"Check at The Bradford Inn front desk. I'm sure it has extras."

"You have inspired me. I will."

Liz explained the history of the buildings they passed. Light snow began to fall. The guide lifted a canvas to cover the riders.

"I assume you don't have a special person in your life since you accepted my invitation tonight. Is that an accurate assumption?"

"Are you questioning me because of the 'Sarah' situation?"

"Just curious."

"I'm single and not dating anyone at the time."

"You're beautiful! Why not?"

"Thank you. Most men I care about are relatives, married, or unpredictable. What about you?"

"I told you that I divorced four years ago. Surely, you've met someone who interests you."

"When I was in college, I had to study because I had not prepared for a business major. With a traveling job, it's hard to have a relationship."

Max responded, "Yeah, that makes sense. I haven't tried to meet anyone. I don't want to experience another divorce."

"I understand. Many of my classmates are in their second marriage. They started happily."

"Is marriage in your life plan, or will you remain a career woman?"

"I haven't written it off!"

"Good. I haven't either, especially since I took my last train ride."

Max winked at Liz. They rode in silence for a few minutes.

"Are you hungry?"

"I always have room for food, and the carolers arc probably singing now," responded Liz.

Max felt differently about this trip to Vermont. He realized Becca had not entered his mind. He and Liz rode in silence until they reached the diner. Before they entered the restaurant, Liz sang with the carolers for a couple of songs. Her soprano voice blended with the others perfectly.

"You have a beautiful voice."

"Thanks. I don't get to practice much, but I enjoy singing. With my schedule, I don't get the opportunity to serenade often. That was fun tonight."

During the meal, they shared stories about dreams and hobbies. They talked for hours. It was like two best friends meeting at a class reunion.

As they walked to the inn, they held hands. Before entering the lobby, Max wrapped his arms around Liz and looked into her eyes. "Any plans for tomorrow?"

"None for the morning. I enjoy the children's excitement when Santa arrives at three."

"Let's meet at nine in the lobby and visit the ski resort. We'll be back by three."

"That sounds good. Max, I had a wonderful time tonight. Thank you."

"I can't believe I am saying this, but I'm glad I'm in Vermont for Christmas."

"I'm glad you're here, too."

Max framed Liz's face with his hands. He gently kissed her. He was happy when Liz responded to his kiss.

"See you in the morning."

"Good night."

Both were reminiscing about their romantic evening. Liz went to the lounge to check with Sam, and Max walked to his apartment. When Liz fell asleep in her comfy bed, her last thoughts were of Max. Her heart was happy. She concluded he might not know good music, but he knew how to kiss.

In his bed, Max lay awake for a while, too. He felt a connection with Liz he had never felt with Becca. Liz was genuine. They had fun together. They communicated on many subjects and listened to each other's opinions. They had similar work ethics and tastes. *Sometimes, a person must marry once before knowing how to pick a wife. I think I have received my Christmas present.*

Max's phone rang. "Hello, Diane."

Diane Harris said, "Oh, Max, the kids loved the snow photos. I had to call and thank you again."

"I'm glad."

"Claire wants us to select the one with the big red ornaments on the street corner for a Christmas card cover next year. She is excited and wants to go to the Bradford Inn for the holidays."

"Diane, it's beautiful here."

"I heard you had a surprise when you arrived."

"Margo told you, huh?"

"Yes, you know she can't keep a secret. Is your ex a problem for your family?"

"No, I probably won't see her again."

"Good. If Claire has her way, the Wildflowers may join you in Wellington for Christmas next year."

"That would be great. However, Wellington will never be the same after that."

"You're right. Listen, have a great holiday. We love you."

Max placed his phone on the side table and looked at the ceiling. *I'm glad I met those ladies. They are the best friends a person can have. I trust those women and Liz!*

That night, Liz and Max's circle of family, friends, and enemies rested and prepared for the next day. Marty and Jill did not check on Max that night. They didn't want to disturb him. The misguided bellhop drove home in wet clothes, sneezing but with no broken bones. He planned to meet with the security chief when the man returned from sick leave. Beautiful Becca spent two hours getting mud out of her glorious hair, and desperate Jake vowed to go to the lounge early tomorrow and wait until he spoke to Liz. All had plans that would impact the lives of others forever.

Chapter 14

Chief Frank Lewis retired from the Wellington Police Department five years ago to become head of security at the inn. It was an easy job until today when a young bellhop presented a notebook of absurd evidence that suggested that current guests might be involved in criminal activity. The chief struggled with a horrendous sinus infection. Nevertheless, he had to investigate.

"Haven't seen you for a few days." Sam greeted the head of security when he entered the hotel lounge.

"I sniffled, went home, took medicine, and slept all afternoon. This morning my sinuses are giving me a fit. My head feels like a block of Styrofoam."

"Sometimes, rest is the best medicine. Why didn't you stay home?"

"I thought I would sit in my office today, but someone brought an issue to my attention. I arranged to meet Annabelle here. I would like you to join the conversation if you don't mind." The chief sneezed several times.

"May I get you anything to drink?"

"A bottle of water, please," answered the chief between sneezes.

"Any problems with security?"

"My head is throbbing. Got any aspirin?"

"Sure."

"We may have a genuine issue. Since I'm foggy due to this sinus situation, I've called other law enforcement to assist me."

"How serious?" Sam reached under the counter and grabbed a bottle of aspirin.

"I don't know, but I must investigate, regardless."

Annabelle arrived, and the chief shared the gist of the information but not all of the details. When he shared the allegation discovered by the new bellhop, Annabelle checked the new employees' section in her hotel workbook.

"I don't mean to act naïve, but this sounds ludicrous. What woman would want to kill a man at Christmas?" Annabelle asked. "The kid is new to the staff. How reliable is he?"

"He witnessed several conversations and took detailed notes. I don't think we can ignore it." The chief sneezed again. "My head feels like cotton."

Sam asked, "What are our options?"

"I informed the sheriff's office and hired four retired men to patrol the corridors and outside the building as a precaution for the next few days. Also, we need to keep this information between the three of us."

Annabelle displayed great concern for the safety of her clientele and her employees. She wanted to know the name of the alleged victim.

The chief answered, "All we know is it's a man. The bellhop provided good details, but nothing led to a name."

The chief did not share the information regarding Sarah or Jake Jones. Only he and the bellhop knew that. Because Jake Jones was an entertainer and misinformation could cause celebrity lawsuits against the inn, the chief withheld that information until he was required to announce it.

"Chief, maybe you need to go home. You sound awful." Annabelle was concerned for her head of security.

"No, I need to handle this. My officers will do everything they can to prevent a murder. The new guys will be wearing blue blazers and have green IDs."

The code name for the operation was Silver Bells. Anyone in the group who found additional information must contact someone with a green ID and say, "Silver Bells." Anyone discovering additional information was to say the code name on the walkie and find Annabelle, the chief, or an individual in a blue blazer. Most team members would meet at nine in the chief's office every morning for updates. The night deputies would meet at six.

Law enforcement did not know the alleged victim's identity, but all knew the future crime scene, The Bradford Inn.

Chapter 15

Sunday morning, the Harvelle family split to work on different tasks. Dan and Charlie shopped for last-minute Christmas gifts, ate a late breakfast, and returned to Dan's suite to watch football bowl games scheduled all day. Max met Liz for an excursion. After Jill and Marty met with Annabelle to finalize the ceremony arrangements, they headed to Becca's suite.

When Jill told Becca about the wedding plans, the ex-daughter-in-law was stunned. Max had shown no interest in her since she arrived. The bride-elect didn't even know where Max was spending the night. She listened to the other two babble about a small, intimate wedding scheduled in two days in the quaint wedding chapel where she had first tied the knot.

"Now, Becca, listen. A local florist will provide a lovely basket arrangement for the stage area and a matching bridal bouquet." Jill was giddy with excitement.

"We've arranged for the inn's notary to perform the ceremony in front of the family. You need to call your parents and arrange for them to fly if you want them present," added Marty.

"The wedding must happen on Tuesday due to scheduling activities at the inn. We were fortunate to schedule it at such a busy time." Jill paused to reflect. "Marty, did we forget anything?"

"I can't think of anything else. Since most guests are on ski trips out of the hotel, no other activities are scheduled for Tuesday."

“Max and I are getting married Tuesday?” asked Becca, not believing it.

“Yes,” said Marty. “Isn’t it wonderful?”

“Are you sure about this?” asked Becca in astonishment.

“Oh, yes,” said Jill. “We’re so excited.”

“And Max is happy about this?” asked Becca. “Are you sure?”

“Absolutely. Dad used the word giddy, didn’t he, Mother?”

“Yes, Max is acting like a schoolboy.”

“I’m glad to hear that,” said Becca, trying to figure out what in the world had happened.

“You don’t look happy, Becca,” said Jill.

“Oh, I am,” Becca responded quickly, with a huge smile. “But I need to clear everything with Max. And I need a beautiful gown, ” agreed Becca, wondering about her surprise wedding.

“Oh, no worries. We have taken care of everything. Annabelle Bradford has arranged a private lunch in a small room for the family after the 11:00 a.m. service,” Marty explained happily.

“That’s different from last time. We ate in the hotel’s formal dining room.” Becca displayed her disappointment. She wanted everyone to see her.

“That area is reserved for the photographer for Santa Claus children’s pictures this year.” Marty understood Becca’s disappointment.

“Well, we can later have a grand party in Orlando for our friends.” Becca faked her excitement.

“You guys can decide on that later, after the honeymoon.” Marty gasped. “We did not think about the honeymoon!”

Jill responded, “I forgot about that, too. I don’t know if Max has planned one or not.”

Becca gladly took over the conversation. “I’m sure Max has planned something wonderful for us. Maybe he will take me to Paris for two weeks. That would be fabulous. However, I must talk to him about several ideas and my plans. Do you happen to know where he is right now?”

Confused about the turn of events, Becca tried not to show it. She couldn’t believe Max had agreed to this plan without talking to her. However, Max was acting weird these days; maybe he loved her. She preferred to converse with him about his investment in her new company. Jill and Marty had moved too fast. She'd much rather get the money her way than marry him.

"Becca, we found the most beautiful dress," said Jill.

Becca assumed Max was moving back to Orlando because he could live anywhere since he worked from home. This time she would insist on a big house in Heathrow, the most exclusive area in the trendy city. Only the rich and famous people lived there. He could update the mother-in-law's suite into a small space for his business.

"Becca?" asked Marty, interrupting Becca's thoughts.

"Huh?"

"Open this box," said Marty, proudly handing the white package to her sister-in-law.

When Marty opened a large box to reveal an atrocious garment, Becca faked her excitement. She couldn't believe she was getting married in that white rag. The outfit had no glam, no style. She didn't remember a dime store on Main Street.

When she realized Jill and Marty were glowing, anticipating her reaction, Becca forced a smile as big as possible. She prayed the tacky costume didn't fit. Then again, she had no money to buy another one.

Becca slowly touched the white material and ran her hands over the dress.

"Please try it on, dear. We can't wait to see it on you."

"Yes, we think it will fit you like a glove," added Marty.

"Okay." *Please let it be too small. What changed Max's mind? They are talking about how happy he is. Giddy like a teenager, they claim. He can't quit smiling! He admits he is the happiest he has ever been. Maybe that little red dress changed his mind. That must be it! It was worth every dollar I spent on it.*

"It fits you perfectly!" said Marty.

"Yes, it does," said Becca as she stared at herself in the full-length mirror on the closet door.

"Take it off. We don't want it wrinkled. One more task completed. We must take care of a few more items on our list." Jill said.

After Jill and Marty left the suite, Becca reflected. It sounded unbelievable, but apparently, her plan had worked without her even trying that hard. It wasn't the dream wedding she deserved, but with the marriage came financial security. She had achieved her goal. She was both thrilled and relieved. Becca thought about calling Max but remembered she did not know his cell phone number or where he was staying. She needed to talk to him. This wedding idea was crazy. How could it happen without Max meeting with her?

"I am getting married in forty-eight hours in an ugly thrift store dress! My wealthy ex-mother-in-law asked me to marry her rich son," said Becca as she threw the piece of cloth in the box.

While Jill and Marty were arranging Max's wedding, he and Liz arrived at the ski resort town of Concord. Liz suggested they visit a little coffee shop that served delicious bagels. Max held her hand as they strolled to the café.

Max and Liz sat in a booth near a large window that provided a beautiful view of the snow-covered mountains. Max shared about his company and his family's Christmas traditions, which reminded Liz of a story of the Cooper family, who came to the inn every year for the holidays.

That's when Max discovered Liz worked for the Bradford Inn. Why had she left out that little detail? She was more private about her life than he had imagined. Maybe he was moving too fast with Liz. She had a kind spirit; a person couldn't disguise that. However, she had secrets.

He remembered Becca had disguised her true feelings and found out too late. He would be a better listener and ask more questions this time. Now he understood why Liz was visiting Jacksonville. After strolling around the town, they returned to the inn in time to watch Santa Claus with the children.

"Would you like to join me in a photo with Santa Claus?" asked Max.

"Sure."

After their holiday photo, Liz and Max helped distribute gifts and led the children to the restaurant for treats. When the chef and volunteers introduced games for the little ones, Max gently kissed Liz and left to join his family and watch football.

Stepping into the elevator, Max recalled the facts he knew about Liz. Jake and Liz had graduated in the same class, had sung together as a duet, had worked as a couple, and had planned to attend college together. Someone in her past had hurt Liz. That's why she had left parts out of her life story. Like Max, Liz had tried to forget those sad times.

Max remembered the incident at the Jake Jones concert. If Jake Jones had hurt her in the past, if he is the reason Liz avoids men, Max confirmed he would destroy every one of Jake Jones' CDs. No wonder she hated country music.

As he walked down the hall to his parents' suite, Max resolved to tell Liz how he felt about her. He liked who he was when he was around her. After that decision, he felt a calm and peaceful feeling. He believed they needed more time together to be sure.

Emerald Eyes had secrets, but Max had a plan. He paused to check his phone calls. No messages. He laughed when he heard Dad and Charlie yelling about the quarterback's Hail Mary! His family loved college football. The game must be exciting today. Later, during the game's halftime, Max's love life became the topic of conversation.

After a few minutes of teasing, Max confessed, "I think I am happier than I have ever been. Sometimes it takes time for people to understand what is best for them. I'm going to meet with her tomorrow."

Dan looked at Jill. When tears rolled down his wife's cheeks, he leaned over and kissed his wife. They recognized their son was in love again and hoped for the best for Becca and him.

"Son, I have a surprise for you. Please, don't make any plans for Tuesday morning." Jill interjected.

"Mother, I don't need any more of your surprises."

"No, this is a good one. Wear your navy suit. Everyone must dress up."

"All of us?" asked Dan.

"Yes, it will be amazing!" declared Jill proudly.

After that, it didn't matter who won the game. Nothing could spoil this gift of Christmas. The Harvelle family felt it was a time for rejoicing because Max was remarrying Beca, the love of his life.

After Max left to return to his lodging, Jill pulled Marty aside to ask if they should call Becca and inform her about Max's plan for tomorrow. Both agreed they should not spoil the surprise. They high-fived each other and hugged.

Dan saw Jill and Marty laughing. He punched Charlie and pointed to their wives. “I’m glad we came here now. Those two are so happy. You and I are having a vacation when you think about it.”

“Yeah, they shop all the time.”

“They are on a mission to help Max find happiness, and we watch all the football we want.”

“I have not had one ‘honey-do’ since we arrived,” said Charlie.

“No cooking, no cleanup,” said Dan

“This is Heaven on Earth,” said Charlie.

“Don’t let Max hear you say that.”

“That’s right. Your son would say Madison County is Heaven on Earth.”

“Yes. As head of the household, I say we make this place our annual Christmas destination.”

“If the girls agree,” Charlie added. “Even Max would approve of that now.”

Dan nodded. “Imagine he and Becca together again. This wedding may be the biggest surprise of the year.”

Charlie lowered his head and looked delighted. He glanced lovingly toward his wife across the room. He was happy for Max and Becca, but the Harvelle family’s most significant present was coming on Christmas morning.

While the Harvelle and Bradford families experienced a casual Sunday, Jake and Becca struggled with situations in their lives. Jake did not have a show on Sunday, so his goal was to talk to Lizzie. He showed his stress as he searched everywhere. The lounge was closed. Even if he found Sam, he would get no information from Lizzie’s buddy. Therefore, he didn’t hunt for Sam. He didn’t know where Lizzie lived. Even the clerk at the main desk provided no information.

When Jake searched for Annabelle, she was in a meeting. When he failed to find Lizzie, he considered his options. Maybe he should send her flowers tomorrow and follow the florist as she delivered them or wait until Lizzie signs for them at the front desk. She would have to talk to him then. But that would cost him money, and what if she wasn't working tomorrow? With his failed mission, he remembered his other option: Becca. He would present his investment opportunity to her as a backup plan.

In Max's suite, Becca focused on Jill and Marty's news. She ordered room service and planned her new house, designing each room. She envisioned her new life in Orlando.

Since Becca had sold her diamond ring years ago, Max must provide a new one. If he hasn't purchased one yet, she would request he wait until they could go together and create a unique signature symbol of their love. Much larger this time. And they would select a diamond bracelet to match to celebrate the second wedding.

Frequently, she remembered yesterday's brawl in the snow, fearing she would get a cold from the horrible incident. She had thrown her gorgeous white and red outfit in the trash. The brat child ruined her expensive designer clothes. And now, she was remarrying Max in a pauper's dress. She would accidentally lose every photo of her in that humiliating costume.

"What did Jill think when she purchased that cotton flour sack for me to wear? Tacky is too good of a word for that hideous dress."

Her cell phone rang, and Becca recognized Jake's number. "Hello, Jake."

"I missed you at the hayride last night."

"Oh, my gosh, I suffered a catastrophic accident. A horrid child ran into me deliberately, and I was shoved violently into a huge, frigid mountain of dirty, dreary snow. I'm sorry I didn't make it to the hayride. I was looking forward to the excursion."

"That sounds terrible. I'm sorry that happened to you."

"It was truly dreadful."

"No broken bones?"

"No, but I know I experienced emotional trauma as a result. I am so disappointed in missing that fun hayride."

"If the time is convenient, I thought I could stop by and share my investment opportunity with you."

"Your timing is perfect. I've ordered room service. Come to suite number 224."

During lunch, Becca embellished the story about her horrendous fall near the inn's entrance. When Jake laughed, Becca saw the humor in the situation. They took turns bragging about their achievements and successes in money management. Jake focused on his singing career and awards. Becca faked an interest in Jake's investment and asked questions that allowed Jake to brag about his expertise in finance. They talked for hours about the potential of investing in Jake's plan.

After the meeting, Becca asked Jake for a prospectus her broker could review. Jake left without a signed document, but he felt confident that Becca had money to burn, and he would get his share of it.

When Jake returned to his suite, he created an investor calculation sheet for Becca. He concluded she was obsessed with making money, and he had said the right words to persuade her to invest in his company. She was beautiful; he wouldn't mind marrying her if he had to, but Lizzie was the most accessible ticket to the cash he needed.

Jake contemplated his strategy. He and Lizzie had an adoration connection. Mostly, she adored him! Tomorrow he would meet with her and do the apology thing. After solving that piece of business, he would insist they marry in the chapel right after Christmas. Of course, he would postpone the honeymoon because he had to return to Nashville.

Jake relaxed on the gray leather sofa and evaluated his situation. "Last night, Lizzie was on the hayride with that Max guy. Why was he with my Lizzie? He cares nothing for her! Poor Lizzie. She never wins. I'll announce my new song on Monday night, but I'll tell both Lizzie and Becca the song is dedicated to each of them. I'll rename it 'My New Love.' It's a perfect setup."

Jake laughed. "Great day in the morning! I may get Lizzie and the dough from Becca if she invests. And I have agreed to do a private concert for Max in the chapel on Tuesday for a reasonable fee. That Harvelle family must be rich. Yep, the new year looks promising – one way or another. CMA, start engraving those trophies with the name Jake Jones!"

At four o'clock, Annabelle needed a break. Although the lounge was closed on Sunday, she knew Sam was working late today. When Sam saw her enter, he had a hunch she was stressed about the chief's investigation. He poured her a glass of wine. She accepted and sipped before she spoke.

"Thanks. I haven't been to any of Jake's concerts yet. How is it going? Still drawing a crowd?"

"The lounge is packed every night. The locals who know Jake return for concerts. Any more news from the chief?"

"Nothing new. I am going crazy over this. To add to the problem, yesterday, a couple decided to get married on Tuesday."

"What happened to your policy about advanced reservation schedules?"

"You know how I feel about weddings. I forgot my policy. The marriage ceremony is small. Won't take more than an hour, including the meal. It's a party of seven or eight, and they were willing to pay the late fee."

Sam knew how hard Annabelle worked and how she loved the inn. He encouraged her to leave the criminal issue to the investigators.

"Nothing may come of the whole situation. What else is bothering you?"

"Sam, have you noticed Liz is smiling more than usual?"

"I haven't seen Liz that much."

"Do you think she and Jake have reconciled?"

"I don't think that is going to happen."

"Sure, it will happen. I think Jake apologized to Liz for what happened after graduation."

"He did?"

"He told me he still loved Liz."

"Jake said those exact words?"

"Not exactly, but that's what he meant."

"Annabelle, is that the reason you gave Jake this gig?"

"Sort of."

Sam placed his hands and elbows on the bar and remained silent.

"Jake said he was sorry and wanted Liz's forgiveness."

"Did you set this up thinking Jake and Liz might reconnect and get married?"

"Yes, she still loves Jake. A mother recognizes the signs of love. Don't tell anyone, but I'm calling a wedding planner."

"On Sunday?"

"Yes, I can't wait until tomorrow. I want the wedding here in the lounge, and the famous musician and my daughter will say their vows on that stage."

"Annabelle?"

"Listen, I saw this in a magazine one time. A couple created a gigantic platform for their wedding in Miami. They built a wooden wedding cake where the bottom tier was the floor. The next layer was even with the stage. The third layer was on top of the second one. There were wooden steps to reach each of the three layers. It looked like a gigantic wedding cake for the bride and groom to stand on."

"Annabelle?"

"It will be spectacular!"

"Annabelle?"

"And you know what comes next? Grandchildren!"

"Why don't you go with me in the morning, and let's get a cute little puppy for you."

"A dog can't call me 'Mimi'!"

"I'm suggesting you not tell anyone about the wedding planner. Don't even research one yet. Just wait until Liz announces her engagement. Be patient. Have some more wine."

"I'm sorry you don't share my joy for my daughter."

"I do. I want Liz to find a great man."

Annabelle stared into Sam's eyes. "What has she said to you?"

"She doesn't confide in me regarding her personal life."

"I don't believe you. Liz tells you everything."

"Not everything."

"My intuition says she will be known as Ms. Liz Jones soon. I feel it so strongly; I will make a bet with you."

"How much?"

"$100 that my daughter marries Jake Jones before the holiday season ends."

"You're on."

"Sam, I hate taking your money. You have another grandbaby on the way."

“Don’t worry. I will enjoy taking yours. I will buy a present for the new one with it.”

The long-time employee shook hands with Annabelle, sealing the deal. After Annabelle left the lounge, Sam chuckled. *Everybody trusts the bartender.*

Chapter 16

Monday morning, Max arrived at the restaurant a few minutes early. Growing more nervous as he waited, he rehearsed what he would say to Liz. When his Emerald Eyes entered, Max stood and pulled her chair out for her. Wow, she's beautiful! He stared at her and forgot to speak.

Finally, Liz broke the silence. "Good morning!"

"Yep, it is, isn't it!"

After a minute of silence, they remembered the restaurant had a breakfast buffet. They laughed at their nervousness and walked to the serving table to select their early meal. Although the food was fabulous, Max could barely eat; he wanted to share his plan.

"Can we talk before we eat?"

"Sure."

"Liz,"

"Yes."

"I have an idea."

She put her coffee down and looked at Max, giving him her full attention. "Okay."

Max took her hand and held it. "For the past four years, I have avoided women. I don't want you to think I'm against marriage. It's just that I'm gun-shy. Does that make sense?"

"I understand."

"You do?"

"Yes."

"Good. Uh, I enjoy being around you. Honestly, I haven't found anything about you I don't like."

"I feel the same way about you."

"Really?"

"Yes."

"Great. We've only known each other for a few days, but I feel connected. Do you?"

"Yes, I do."

"Good. I know I messed up with my first choice of a marriage partner. I don't know about your former relationships, but we must be careful this time. Do you agree?"

"Yes, I think that is important."

"I propose we date each other exclusively. Because my job allows me the freedom to work from anywhere with Internet access, I am willing to move here, or you can move to Florida for a while. That will give us time to determine if this is love or infatuation with those emerald eyes." He picked up his coffee cup and took a long breath. "What do you think of that idea?"

"Can you be a little more specific?"

"Sure. My home is on a beautiful lake; we can live there or find you an apartment in Madison County. Margo, one of the Wildflowers, is a real estate agent who will help us. Sydnee, another Wildflower, owns a bed-and-breakfast where you can stay."

"Those sound like good options."

"I could travel with you if you like that idea when you travel to other states for extended periods."

"You've thought about everything."

He paused for a long minute. "You will always be Liz. You would never have to be Sarah again."

Liz looked tenderly at Max.

"Oh, and I will stop listening to country music if that will help your decision."

Liz laughed and reached with her other hand. "I haven't been this happy in a long time. I like who I am when I am with you. I don't quite understand it because I've never experienced this feeling."

"I know. When I'm not with you, I can't stop thinking about you."

"Yes, Max. That's it, and I can't stop smiling."

"So, what do you think?"

"I had planned to work out of Florida for a while. If we can work out the logistics, I think we should do this."

Max stood and went around the table. He placed his hand under her chin and kissed Liz gently. "You have made me a happy man today."

He returned to his seat. "Whew! Maybe I can eat now."

"Me, too."

Max ate everything on his plate while he shared the beauty of Cherry Lake, Madison County, and the Wildflowers. "I can't wait for you to meet these three women who have become my extended family. They have an interesting history; you will love them. Sydnee and JJ's wedding date is February 14th. Please add that event to your calendar."

After a delicious meal, Liz headed to the office conference room for the weekly leadership team meeting. She bounced with enthusiasm even though she was last on the agenda today. All she could think about was her conversation with Max.

Too excited to return to his suite, Max walked to the nearest jewelry store. He purchased a gold necklace with an emerald pendant, dangling earrings to match, and a gorgeous gold bracelet. He planned to give them to Liz as a Christmas gift.

As Max left the store, he stopped outside and remembered something important about the new woman in his life. He spent a chunk of change on his sweetheart and did not know her last name! *I must be crazy in love!*

While Max shopped for the love of his life, his mother and Marty spent the day reviewing all the plans for the surprise wedding. When they could not reach Becca, they assumed she was at breakfast with Max. They briefly met with the inn photographer and then spent the day shopping for unique gifts to remind a happy couple of the pending nuptials.

They also checked on the bridal bouquet at the floral shop, which would deliver everything to the chapel at 10:00 a.m. Jill and Marty enjoyed reminiscing about the happy couple and looked forward to the years ahead.

"Marty, our family is growing by one. I'm so happy for Max."

Marty embraced her mother and squeezed her. "Yes, it's going to be a great family Christmas."

Annabelle, dressed in her company holiday red blazer, entered the boardroom for the administrative meeting. Sam submitted the financial report for the lounge for the past week and left the meeting early when a delivery truck arrived. Chef proudly revealed the latest health department report and the menu suggestions for January. Liz presented an overview of her recent recruiting trip. The boss concluded the meeting by reviewing the weekly activities calendar and announced an additional wedding for Tuesday.

As Annabelle left the room, she glanced down the hall and gave a thumbs-up to the visitor waiting. *Oh, he is waiting for his fiancé. How sweet! Maybe they will inform me today. And again, I know more about love than Sam.*

Liz was the last to leave the meeting because she had to disconnect her computer due to the PowerPoint presentation. As she left the room, a man sat in a chair in the hallway waiting for her. He held a green vase filled with beautiful yellow roses with deep green, lacy ferns. She didn't speak. What shocked her most was that she did not drop anything or act clumsily. She felt calm.

"Jake?"

"Hey. I waited for you for over an hour. That's how important you are to me."

"Our administration meetings usually last all morning." Liz added, "You got a break today."

"Can we go inside the board room and talk briefly?"

"For a few minutes? Sure."

After they sat, Liz asked. "How did you know about the board meeting this morning?"

"I called Annabelle yesterday."

"I see."

"Did Sam miss the meeting?" asked Jake.

"No, he was here but had to leave early."

"Good. Oh, these are for you. The vase reminded me of your beautiful eyes." Jake pushed the vase in front of her.

She didn't touch the vase or examine the flowers.

"Lizzie."

"I prefer to be called Liz now."

"Okay, Liz, I need to say something to you. I should have said this a long time ago. I sincerely apologize for how I treated you, especially when I left you after graduation. I wanted to tell you when we were on the carriage ride that night, but you were excited and babbling about college. I didn't want to make you sad."

"I understand. I accept your apology."

"What?"

Jake couldn't think for a minute, caught off guard by that comment. That was too soon for him; he had prepared to grovel. Her attitude shocked him. He became agitated but quickly refocused and regained his fake apologetic composure.

"Lizzie, I mean, Liz, I am truly sorry for how I acted."

"It's okay. I have no hard feelings."

"You don't hate me?"

"Of course not; I forgot all about it."

"But you avoid me."

"I don't need to see you. I am focused on my new job."

"No one will give me your phone number when I ask. I assume people are following your instructions."

"That is accurate."

"So, you are angry with me!"

"I was hurt, but I've moved on. You don't need my phone number. Sam oversees the lounge now."

"Would you at least sing with me one more time?"

Shaking her head, "No."

"Well, how about lunch?" asked Jake. "I know you must eat. We could catch the bus to the ski resort and go to that little café you like. I want to spend some quality time with you while I am here."

"I love that little place, but I spent the day there yesterday. Had a wonderful time."

"Well, one of the projects I'm working on while home for the holidays is speaking to potential clients who would benefit from my professional success. Lizzie, I mean Liz, this opportunity is the chance of a lifetime. I want to share it with the people I love back home. Would you consider being an investor in my company?"

"My broker manages all my investments."

"I understand, but I'm going places. This deal is a sure thing."

"My portfolio is doing well."

"I haven't told anyone, but most of the songs on my next album are about you. I plan to debut one of them at tomorrow night's show. It would mean so much to me if you were there."

"I have engagements for the next three nights."

"How convenient for you. The fact that you are avoiding me says you are angry with me, doesn't it?"

Liz stood up. "Absolutely not. I have fond memories of high school."

"Me, too. I remember those good times we had. I have never stopped loving you."

"I wish you the best, Jake, but if you think your future will include me, it won't happen. You're the music man. I'm the businesswoman."

"Please give me a chance to show you I have changed. We made a good team."

"I've moved on. You should, too."

"I'm not giving up. I will always love you. Nothing will ever change that."

"I'll tell my children when they see your picture in one of those entertainment magazines, 'I sang with that guy in high school.'" She picked up her computer.

"Just in case you change your mind about the investment, I made a projection sheet for you to consider."

Liz accepted the paper and left the room. She focused on her walk and headed out of the building. When she reached the chilly air, Liz was thankful. She wanted to scream, but she held her composure. *Please let me get to my apartment. Mrs. Annabelle told Jake about the administrative meeting. Bless my mother's sweet little heart. He finally cornered me. Jake is like a fly that continues to buzz around a piece of pie.*

After entering her condo, she took a deep breath. She placed her computer on her desk. She grabbed a bottle of water and sat on her sofa. She knew Jake didn't love her, but why did he give her an investment chart? She examined the financial opportunity and realized Jake was selling shares to his own company. The country music star may not be as successful as he claimed. He needed money, not a wife.

Liz threw the investment proposal into the nearest trashcan. Looking at her computer and presentation materials on her desk, Liz realized everything was neatly ordered. She had dropped nothing when encountering Jake Jones!

THE BRADFORD INN BOARDROOM

Staring at the expensive floral bouquet, Jake sat for several minutes, contemplating the meeting with his high school sweetheart. Lizzie was pretending to be confident. He could manage her. She was playing hard to get. *Yeah! She loves me. She went on the hayride with a total stranger to make me jealous. That is hilarious! She's playing a game she can't handle. Poor pathetic Lizzie! It won't be long before she'll come running and beg me to marry her.*

Chapter 17

Tuesday was the scheduled Harvelle wedding at The Bradford Inn. The bride-to-be finally awakened and made a reservation for an early morning massage at the hotel. She charged it to Max's room. Since Max had agreed to marry her again, she rationalized he wouldn't mind pampering her. She didn't understand why Max had not asked her personally, but she trusted Jill. Becca headed downstairs and ate breakfast at the café on the mezzanine. She turned off her cell phone and entered the spa.

While Becca prepared for her wedding, Liz found her mother reviewing the day's schedule. Since most hotel guests were having fun at the ski resort in Hampton, very few people remained at the inn. When Liz entered, Annabelle saw the glow on Liz's face and put her glasses on the desk.

"What news do you have? You are beaming!"

"I have something to tell you. Are you too busy right now?"

"Never too busy for my daughter."

"I may have found my soul mate. He is handsome, kind, sweet, and a great kisser." Her face was blushing. She over-gestured with her hands.

"Oh, I had a feeling this would happen." Annabelle stood and hugged her daughter. "Tell me everything."

"We had a great talk this morning. We settled the logistics between us."

Annabelle asked, "Have you told Sam about this yet?"

"No."

"Are you positive he is the one?"

"Yes."

"I am happy about this news. When you tell Sam, make sure you say you told me first. Got it?"

"Okay, I'm going there next."

After Liz left her office, Annabelle called her son in Paris. "Bryan, good morning!"

"Mother? Is everything okay? Is anybody sick?"

"No, why do you ask that?"

"Remember the time difference?"

"Sweetheart, I am sorry. I was excited; I didn't think." Annabelle looked at the clock on the wall. "Wait a minute; it's 3 p.m. in Paris. Were you in bed asleep?"

"Yes."

"Are you sick? Why aren't you in class this afternoon?"

"It's winter break. Remember?"

"I'm too excited. Forgive me."

"It's okay. I'm resting because I'm participating with the school community service team serving at a soup kitchen tonight. It's one of the annual events during the holidays the college supports. I was enjoying a deserved nap."

"I love what the college is doing. I'm proud of you."

"Thanks. Are you calling about a recipe?"

"No. I have wonderful news. Liz and Jake are getting married."

"Liz is marrying Jake Jones?" Bryan threw the bedspread off and stood up.

"Yes!"

"This doesn't make sense. My sister loathes Jake."

"They resolved those issues. Liz just told me right here in the office. Can you come home for the wedding?"

"They are moving that fast? This reconciliation is hard to believe." Bryan walked toward the kitchen to get a bottle of juice.

"Yes, I'm sure Jake has to return to Nashville. If you can't come, I will put the ceremony on Zoom. Liz will understand, sweetheart."

"I'm not going to miss my sister's wedding. I'll check with the airlines and see what's available."

"Okay. You know what else this means?"

"No, what?"

"You are off the hook for another year or two. Liz will give me grandbabies. But I expect you to get down to business three years from now."

"Remember, when Liz has babies, she won't be traveling for the inn."

"I will hire a nanny and keep them in my office while she travels."

"I'm not sure she will agree to that plan."

"Liz does not have to give up her career when she and Jake get married."

"What day is Liz getting married?"

"We will plan it for the day after you arrive! So, let me know when you are leaving Paris."

"And you are sure this marriage is going to happen?"

"Yes! Which reminds me, have you found a colleague who sparks your interest?"

"I have."

"Bryan, why didn't you tell me? Listen, bring her home with you, and we can have a double wedding. Oh, I have so much to do to get things organized. I've never had the opportunity to do a double wedding, but it can't be that hard. Now, I will definitely hire a wedding planner."

"Mrs. Annabelle, stop!"

"Okay?"

"The lady who sparks my interest is thirty years older than me."

"Who is this old Jezebel trying to steal my young son? I'm coming over there!"

"She's my instructor, and I love her because I am learning French culinary skills."

"Bryan, I will confine you to your condo when you come home for scaring me that way."

"I couldn't resist. I love you, Mother."

"I love you, too, but don't scare me that way again!" Annabelle caught her breath. "I forgot to tell you. I rented your suite."

"Why?"

"I don't know. Sam requested it. The inn had no vacancies, and the man needed a room."

"My stuff is in there."

"The staff removed all the important articles and your pictures. They rolled in a garment hanger so the guest would have closet space."

"Okay, how long will the person live in my apartment?"

"I don't know; I didn't ask."

"Since I am coming home, I think it's a good question."

"I will, but you may have to stay with me. Let me know when you are arriving. I want this to be a surprise for Liz."

"I will try to schedule a flight."

"Thank you. See you soon. Love you, sweetheart."

Annabelle cleared her desk and grabbed a notebook. *Next, hire a wedding planner. Liz's dress must be spectacular because the wedding photos will be in celebrity magazines. I wonder what Vera Wang has available?* Then she remembered her bet with Sam. *And I have an extra one hundred dollars to spend. Nothing can make me sad now.*

When Jill and Marty knocked on Max's suite to get Becca, no one answered. They exchanged glances. They hated to wake the lovebirds, but it was two hours before the wedding.

"They may be eating breakfast," suggested Marty.

"Max rises early. He should be back in his suite by now. You don't think they eloped? Remember, he said he would announce his plan to her at breakfast?"

"Maybe we should have told him last night about the wedding ceremony scheduled at the chapel," Marty worried.

Jill gasped. "If they don't get married at the chapel, we have a major issue."

The bellhop stepped out of the second-floor elevator and heard the last part of the conversation between Jill and Marty.

"What?" Marty exclaimed.

"The man will be livid if he has paid all that money."

"Oh, yeah."

Jill blurted out, "Dan will die!"

"Do we have a plan C in case the event does not go as planned?"

"No, it had better happen."

The bellhop turned around, stepped back into the elevator, and immediately called the security chief.

Jill and Marty walked into elevator number two. When they arrived on the first floor, they headed to the lobby and grabbed a continental breakfast with coffee. Marty called the future bride again when they sat down on one of the benches, but all she could get was voice mail.

Jill, growing more frantic, called Max on his cell phone. "Son, Marty and I are near the lobby having a light breakfast in the coffee machine's corridor. Do you want to join us for coffee?"

"Sure, I'm leaving the jewelry store near the inn. Be there in about two minutes."

"Great, dear. See you in a few minutes." Jill, jubilant from that news, hugged Marty. "He has purchased the ring! Everything appears to be falling into place. Why don't you go to your suite and get that lovely wedding dress and accessories laid out for Becca? Keep calling her. You manage her and get her to the chapel by 10:50 a.m. I will get Max dressed and the men down to the venue by the appropriate time for photos."

Max strolled up as Marty was leaving. She hugged her brother and headed to the elevator.

Max stared as she walked away quickly. "What's wrong with her?"

"Oh, nothing, Son. You are already in your suit. You look so handsome."

She looked at the jewelry bag. "What's in the bag?"

"Mom, you know, I told you I planned to ask someone a special question at breakfast this morning?"

"Yes, and did you?"

"She said, 'Yes.'"

Jill squealed. "I am so happy for you, Son. Didn't I tell you this is a season for miracles? Christmas is about love! We'll celebrate at lunch."

Max responded, "I don't know her schedule. She may not be able to meet the family at lunch."

"Don't worry. Your mother takes care of everything. Let's head upstairs. We need to see if Dan is ready, and I must change into my new outfit. I'm so glad you are in your suit already. This day will be one the family will never forget."

The nervous bellhop stood near the elevator, pointed to Jill, and whispered to the security officer in the blue blazer, who stepped into the elevator after Jill and Max entered. Everyone got off on the second floor. The new deputy walked toward the end of the hallway but stopped after Jill and Max entered Dad's suite.

The man on duty reported to the chief the location of the possible perpetrator and the possible victim: Jill Harvelle and her husband, Dan. Once security confirmed the information, Operation Silver Bells went into action.

Annabelle received a call immediately. She informed Chief Lewis the family at the top of his suspect list had reserved the chapel for a wedding at 11:00 a.m. today. She told the chief only a few family members were attending the event and that Jake Jones would provide entertainment. After the ceremony, lunch followed in the small room next to the chapel. She added that the wedding was a hasty request at the last minute.

When the head of security heard those details, he realized all the puzzle pieces fit perfectly. It appeared the nutty bellhop was right. As the chief sneezed, he was thankful this was turning out to be an easy case. He called for backup from the sheriff's office. He placed security in all areas: elevators, hallway, chapel, and small dining room. Chief Lewis had every angle covered if someone attempted a crime in the chapel.

While undercover officers moved to assigned hidden positions, members of the Harvelle wedding party prepared for the day's event. Becca finally turned her phone on, listened to the urgent message from Marty, and ran to Marty's suite. She focused in disbelief as Marty updated her on everything and told her the wedding was about to happen.

Marty exclaimed, "Max purchased the rings this morning!"

"I'm a little confused?"

Marty was so excited about the wedding she wasn't listening to Becca. "Every bride is on her wedding day. Besides, Max told us this morning it was all settled. He is so excited."

"But I would like to talk to Max."

"We don't have time. We scheduled the ceremony for 11:00 a.m. Hurry! Mother has everything ready,"

When Marty brought out the hanger and helped Becca dress, Becca cringed but forced a positive reaction when she looked at the ugliest wedding dress she had ever seen.

Marty assisted Becca with her makeup and hair. The only item Becca loved was the beautiful shoulder-length lacy veil draped around her face. When Becca looked in the mirror, Marty handed her a red silk bridal bouquet. Becca looked stunning.

As Marty swept her eyes down Becca's attire, she realized she had forgotten shoes.

"No problem," said Becca. She ran to her hotel room and pulled out her red high-heeled shoes that matched her sexy red dress. Like Christmas magic, the red colors were identical.

Now completely dressed, Becca looked at her reflection in the full-length mirror. "I hope Max purchased a huge diamond. It doesn't matter; I will choose what I want later. Mrs. Harvelle, you are back in high society and will get everything you deserve. Max is lucky to get me."

As Becca entered the hallway to meet Marty, she practiced her bridal smile. She wanted everyone to admire her as she entered the lobby. *I can't believe my crazy plan worked. Here I am, the bride, perfect and beautiful. Every woman is jealous of me. Maybe guests won't notice this vile dress. They will be looking at my perfect face. What was I thinking? I look good in anything!* Becca snickered. *I always get what I want.*

When Jill, Max, Dan, and Charlie entered the narthex of the chapel, Jill peeked inside to witness a busy scene. Annabelle conferred with security and a chef while the staff worked. A photographer moved around the room, checked for light exposure, and talked to the tech director, who controlled the stage lighting. At the stage's back right corner, Jake Jones strummed his guitar. The notary, who was short in stature, found his position for the service and sat on the front row near the piano, reviewing his notes. One security guard entered through the back door and walked toward the narthex.

Jill was unaware that undercover officers were already in place. She found the boutonniere tray and pinned all the men before glancing into the venue.

Annabelle noticed the door slightly open and walked toward the narthex. She turned around to inform everyone in the room the party had arrived. Annabelle stepped into the entryway to greet the family.

When the Harvelle family entered the chapel, the photographer snapped casual photos. When Max saw the camera, he realized the big surprise was a family portrait. What a great idea! The Bradford Inn provided an opportunity for Christmas photos for their guests.

"That's a beautiful flower arrangement stand on the stage. The people at this inn think of everything." Max wondered why Jake Jones was in the chapel.

"Yes, they do," answered his mother.

"Mrs. Harvelle, what poses do you want?"

"Let's take a photo of all the men first."

"Okay. Why don't you gentlemen stand in front of the flower stand?"

Dan, Charlie, and Max followed instructions and posed on the stage.

"That's it," The photographer looked toward Jill for further instructions.

"I'll join the photo next," instructed Jill.

"Great."

"Mother, let him take a picture of you and Dad," suggested Max.

"Of course, Son."

"Beautiful. What next?" asked the photographer.

"Max, why don't you have a photo of you leaning against the grand piano?" suggested Jill.

"Okay."

After that shot, Max asked his idol, "Hey, Jake, would you have your picture taken with me?"

"Yeah."

Jake left his guitar on the floor and posed with Max. Afterward, Jake grabbed his guitar and invited all the men for a picture. Dan and Charlie were happy to oblige.

"Thanks, Man. That made my Christmas. The last picture? My dad and Charlie will treasure it. I promise you that."

"Glad to do it."

"Are we interrupting your rehearsal?"

"Your mother asked me to do a small private concert for you."

"She what?"

"I'm singing for you, Max!" Jake returned to the corner.

Max walked to his mom and hugged her. "I don't know how much this cost, but it's my best Christmas present ever."

"You're welcome, Son. I'm so happy for you." Jill continued with instructions for the photographer. "When Marty arrives, which will be soon, I want you to take a picture of her and Charlie together and then one of us as a family."

"Sounds like a good plan." The photographer continued snapping photos.

When Marty walked into the chapel, the photographer grabbed the group and arranged the final family photo and one of Charlie and his wife. Max walked to the far-right side of the chapel, sat in the front row, leaned back, and gave Jake a thumbs up. Max was beaming. He took a deep breath and waited for his private concert to begin.

"Jake, does the lounge have a matinee today?" asked Max.

"No, dude, I'm here just for you." Jake sang one short ballad.

Annabelle went to the center of the stage and asked everyone to be seated. She looked toward the person in the sound booth in the back of the chapel and then at Jake, who played his guitar and sang a second love song.

As Jake crooned one of Max's favorites, the notary took his position before the impressive white floral basket. When he saw how beautiful the bride looked when she entered the chapel, the notary was stunned and forgot to ask the guests to stand.

Max was enthralled with Jake Jones's music and did not hear the chapel door open, and he never noticed the little guy standing on the small stage. Max closed his eyes and listened to the music. *I'm sorry Liz is missing this. The sound in this room is fabulous. I will shop again and get my mom something special. A private concert by Jake Jones is the biggest surprise of my life.*

Chapter 18

The wedding venue was simple but elegant. The red carpet matched the bride's vibrant bouquet of red and white roses. The lone basket of white flowers on the small stage completed the decorations.

Becca strolled gracefully down the aisle in her wedding finery and stood by the notary. No one stood in the groom's place to greet her.

After Jake finished his song, Max sat in reflection. Jake quietly strummed the guitar, waiting for Max to proceed to the stage. When Max opened his eyes, he noticed Becca waiting on the platform.

Max observed his family smiling at Becca. *I can't believe what I am seeing. Is Jake marrying Becca? Gosh, I need to warn him about that woman. Why did Mom think I would want to see this?*

When Jake continued to play, Max's thoughts were confirmed. *Oh my gosh, Jake must be having second thoughts! I don't blame him. Don't do it, man.*

Max waited for Jake to respond. *Run while you can, man! Don't marry that woman.*

"Aren't you going to join me, sweetheart?" whispered Becca.

Max waited until Jake stopped playing his guitar. He never heard Becca speak. He glanced toward his mother, who looked pleased. Dad nodded his head in agreement and gave Max a thumbs up. Marty and Charlie beamed with happiness.

Becca spoke louder. "Aren't you going to join me, sweetheart?"

The notary, growing impatient, asked, "Will the groom step forward, please?"

Max leaned forward and looked at poor Jake. *Becca tried to trap him, and he's just figuring it out.*

At this point, Max realized everyone was looking at him, not Jake.

"Sir, who is the groom?" asked Max, allowing Jake to leave the chapel.

The notary looked at his paper and answered, "I have the name Andrew Maxwell Harvelle as the groom."

"Me? Marry Becca? I don't know where you got my name!" Max walked toward the stage to check the paper with the groom's name. "I'm in love with Liz."

Annabelle shrieked, "You want to marry my daughter, and you proposed to this woman? You are a two-timing jerk. You will break my baby's heart. I will never allow it. Never! Never! Besides, she loves someone else."

Annabelle ran to the piano on the stage, grabbed a candelabra, and pushed toward Max.

Holding his guitar, Jake rose quickly and asked Annabelle, "Who is she in love with?"

Hearing that absurd remark, Annabelle stopped and yelled to Jake, "You!"

"What? No, this is not right. Max, you love Becca," Jill firmly piped up. "You better not touch my Max." She ran toward Annabelle, tripped on the carpet, and hit her head on the stage steps.

Marty exclaimed, "Mom!"

Charlie grabbed his wife. "Sweetheart, please calm down."

"Charlie, my mother is lying on the floor, passed out. She hit her head. Somebody call a doctor. No, call an ambulance. Let me go, Charlie."

"Please calm down. Someone will call a doctor!"

"Who is calling an ambulance? Get out of my way. I need to help my mother!"

Dan ran to check on his wife. Hearing the commotion, an undercover cop came out of hiding, grabbed Dan, and pulled him to the back of the chapel. Two men in uniforms entered from another side door and surrounded Mr. Harvelle for his safety. Dan tried to break free to return to Jill. One person informed Charlie to remain in his seat. Another grabbed Marty and forced her to sit by her husband. Max headed to his mother but saw Annabelle rushing his way. He covered his head with his arms in preparation for a hit.

Dan shouted, "I must see about my wife! She may not be breathing. Can't you see she's passed out? She may have internal injuries. Someone, take care of my wife. Please let me go."

The photographer frantically took pictures of all the action. Security grabbed the cameraman and made him lie on the small stage with his hands on his head. The shutterbug threatened to sue.

Dan begged, "Officer, I must go to my wife."

"Sir, we have to protect you. Someone is trying to kill you."

"Are you crazy? What are you talking about?" Dan lost control and pushed the man back.

Annabelle was too angry to talk to anyone. She headed for the tall man in the front row.

Becca yelled, "Max, what do you mean? I'm heartbroken. I'm humiliated. I'm devastated. I will never forgive you for this." She leaned over and cried loudly, moving into Annabelle's path.

Annabelle pushed Becca out of her way, knocking her into the short notary, but he caught her in his hands.

Max dodged the crazy woman running toward him. "Becca, I don't know what you are talking about."

Max saw Annabelle lose her balance and stop. She then continued to pursue him. "Lady, I don't know your daughter. What is going on here? I don't understand what is happening!"

Annabelle continuously yelled and proceeded on the warpath, following Max around the room. A deputy knocked the weapon out of Annabelle's hands and wrapped his arms around her to stop her.

"Mom, are you okay?" shouted Max, moving toward her.

"No, she is not! Somebody check on my mom. Please," cried Marty.

"Marty, what is all of this about?" asked Max.

"You're marrying Becca today!" said Marty over the noise.

"No, I'm not; I love someone else."

Jake freaked out, dropped his guitar, and sneaked toward Max from behind. "You are not marrying my girl!"

While Max focused on his mother, Jake hit Max's head from the back. Max toppled over and tried to defend himself from Jake's punches. Blood poured from Max's head.

Marty fell to her knees and whimpered, "What? You said you had made a big decision." She fell to the floor, crying hysterically. She hyperventilated and rolled on her back.

One cop ran to Jill on the floor. Another rushed to Marty. Annabelle fought her security protector, managed to escape him, and rushed toward Max again. She intended never to let that sorry human being ever get up.

Becca cried, putting on a show of despair. "Nobody wants to marry me! Can't you see I'm beautiful? You, stupid men, are all blind. Somebody needs to love me! Me! What about me? What about me?" She wailed despondently.

Humiliated, Becca jerked away from the arms of the notary and began her exit from the chapel. But the notary had the same idea. They collided, and Becca lost her balance and fell on the short man, causing him to stumble into the standing, white floral arrangement. Cold water surged from the flower stand, streaming on Becca and the notary.

Becca screamed from the icy water ruining her veil and dress, "My dress, my shoes, my life…all ruined. Ruined! Does anyone in this room care?"

The notary said, "I do."

Becca sputtered, "Oh, shut up!"

Hearing the uproar, cops rushed into the room from every door and hiding place, guns drawn, looking for weapons, and grabbing people. One got hold of Annabelle again and forced her out of the room through the back door.

"Ma'am, please don't make me arrest you. You cannot assault anyone."

She yelled as loud as she could so Max could hear her. "This is not over!"

An investigator handcuffed Jake and forced him to sit on the stage. "Don't move from this spot, or I will take you to jail."

Seeing blood flowing from Max's head, the officer ran to him. The man removed his light jacket and placed it under Max's head. Dark bloodstains formed on the carpet.

"Why aren't you putting handcuffs on that guy? He's the jerk. Arrest him for stealing my girl, breaking Becca's heart, and anything else you can think of," shouted Jake.

Seeing people with weapons, the notary grabbed Becca and dragged her behind a chair, destroying the rest of the wedding bouquet.

The notary whispered to Becca, "These men have weapons."

Becca squealed. "They have guns! Please don't shoot me. They are going to kill us. We're going to perish in this chapel. I don't want to die. Somebody help us."

Everyone hollered after Becca's announcement and tried to leave the room. Cops chased and hand-cuffed as many as they could. When Marty heard the word "weapons," she grabbed Charlie and bolted down the aisle.

One undercover detective secured the chapel entry door. Security stopped her. "Dad, they're holding us hostage!" Marty screamed.

Everyone in the wedding party panicked and searched for an exit again. Becca and the notary crawled slowly under the pews to reach the main entrance. Hearing Marty scream, Annabelle returned to the chapel and took advantage of the situation. The angry owner of the hotel aimed for Max again. However, a law enforcement person pulled Annabelle to the grand piano and handcuffed her to the leg.

Annabelle yelled, "Do you know who I am? I own this inn. I demand you take these barbaric shackles off. I want everyone in this chapel arrested and jailed, especially that Max person and his whole family. All of you are going to be incarcerated for a long time. Do you hear me?"

Annabelle tried to pick up the leg to pull the cuffs away. "Listen, I know you don't make a lot of money. I will pay you to beat that man up" Annabelle stared at Max as she begged a guard.

"Ma'am, I work for the police department. I could charge you for offering a bribe to an officer of the law."

"This lawman threatened to arrest me," Annabelle shouted. "I don't care. My daughter is worth it."

"Ma'am, I don't know who your daughter is!" yelled Max as he pulled himself up from the floor.

Jake begged for his life. "If you're here to kidnap me because I am famous, I don't have any money. I can't pay for bail. I have a concert tonight. Choose someone else."

"Sweetheart, please sit down. You must be careful. Remember?" Charlie looked at his wife.

"Is my wife alive?" yelled Dan from the corner of the chapel. "Sweetheart, can you hear me?"

The chief yelled, "Place handcuffs on Jill Harvelle. Check every woman's purse."

Marty screamed when she heard the chief and hit the officer holding her. "Don't touch my mother!"

Dan tried to get away from those holding him. "No, you can't do that. My wife needs a doctor. All she did was plan a wedding."

The notary remained under the pew and prayed. "Lord, please hear me. We are hostages. Our lives are in danger. Please protect us. And I will never run around on my wife again if you will save me."

A cop got on the walkie-talkie and called for another paramedic. Another one read the Miranda rights to Jake and then to the photographer. Someone assisted Max as he attempted to stop the bleeding from his head. Another deputy stood in front of Dan to guard him. Dan protested, saying he needed to help his wife.

The officer would not allow him to move. "Sir, your life may be in danger!"

"What are you talking about?" Dan shouted to his wife, "Jill, honey, are you okay? Talk to me."

"Are we being arrested? It's Christmas!" moaned Jill.

The paramedics entered the room and assisted Jill first. Then they checked Max's injuries and Marty's. However, the paramedic had to leave Marty to help calm Becca, who was screaming under a pew. Dan Harvelle asked questions and demanded an explanation regarding why the mafia assassins were at his son's wedding.

Finally, the chief yelled, "Quiet!! Now!! We are not holding anyone hostage. We are law enforcement here on duty."

After the wedding party calmed down, the police finally gained control. With a bad headache, Max sat quietly, and Jill breathed better. Becca wept softly. Dan was under the protection of law enforcement and was not allowed to join the others.

Jake asked, "Am I under arrest?"

"I can't give you an answer yet," yelled the chief, pulling out a handkerchief to wipe his nose.

"Can I please have my camera back?" begged the photographer.

"No, we must take it downtown. You can pick it up later," answered the chief as he sneezed and rubbed his forehead.

Jill, who was sitting on the floor now, called for Becca. She spoke sternly, not raising her voice. "This is all your fault, Becca. You tricked me."

"No, I did not! I am innocent. This wedding was all your idea."

"That is not true, and you know it. You are not to contact any member of my family. My son is finished with you, and so are we. Your despicable actions caused this. What a Christmas kerfuffle! We may all go to jail!"

"Sweetheart?"

"I'm okay, Dan. I'm so sorry. Why am I in handcuffs?"

"I want everyone to gather in front and have a seat," said the chief, and he sneezed. "Now, settle down, and let's get quiet. I must sort this situation out."

A guard announced, "All purses are clear. No weapons on the premises, Sir."

Becca whispered to Max, "Please allow me the opportunity to explain what happened. Your mother and sister are confused."

Jill commanded, "Do not speak to my son! I promise you will regret it." Max's mother noticed an officer standing next to her.

"Ma'am, I suggest you not threaten the bride-to-be. You're in enough trouble already."

The chief waited again for cooperation. "Good. Okay, I am Chief Lewis, head of security at the inn. No one is permitted to leave the room until this investigation is over and we have all the answers."

Every suspect except Dan gathered on the front pew. They murmured their displeasure at the situation.

"Stop talking," ordered the chief.

The communication within the group ceased.

"This has been an interesting day. But first on the agenda is identifying the reprobate lodging here without registration. Now, which one of you is Sarah?'" Then he sneezed loudly several times.

Chapter 19

Liz heard the call on the walkie-talkie in her office for Silver Bells in the hotel chapel. She had no clue what that meant. Fortunately, most of the guests were out of the building today. Two security guards had secured the chapel and forbade her to enter when she arrived.

"Sir, I am one of the owners of the inn."

"Ma'am, my orders are to allow no one to enter."

Liz watched as a paramedic arrived and passed through security. She again appealed to the guards. She tried to reach Annabelle by phone.

"Officer, is there anyone I need to call? Like the Chief or an ambulance?"

"Ma'am, the Chief is inside."

"What happened in the chapel? Why doesn't my mother answer her phone?"

"Ma'am, I am not at liberty to answer your questions at this time."

Liz paced for a while. Then, she pulled a chair from the lounge and sat near the chapel for over two hours.

"Ma'am, the doors are about to be opened. You cannot enter until all have exited the area."

"I understand."

Liz stood there anxiously waiting. She recognized the inn's notary and photographer when they left the room. Then, a lady in a wet, dirty white dress exited. She held a soaked veil in her hands. When Liz looked closer, she gasped. That's Max's ex-wife! Her hair was tangled and wet. She carried a pair of red shoes and picked leaves out of her hair. What was she doing in the chapel?

Liz waited patiently for her mother. Four people she did not recognize exited the chapel door. The two women wiped their tears quietly while two gentlemen consoled them. They walked like they were walking on slippery ice. One of the women had a massive bandage on her forehead and a glazed look on her face.

The paramedic bounced out, smiling and shaking her head. She spoke briefly to the security guard outside and walked down the corridor. Then, Jake Jones strutted boldly from the chapel like he owned the place, carrying his guitar.

When he saw Lizzie, he grabbed her and kissed her hard. Jake knew Max was following him out of the chapel. He wanted Max to witness the long kiss.

When Max saw the affectionate caress, he retreated into the chapel and asked for another exit. Today, he discovered another lie about his Emerald Eyes. She was a piece of work. She was not on Christmas vacation. She not only worked at the inn; she was part-owner. She had time to tell him everything about her life but chose not to. Max was wrong. Liz was a better actress than Becca.

Now, he had proof. Annabelle said Liz was in love with Jake, and that kiss said it all. Now, he understood all those phone calls from Becca.

Liz pushed Jake away. "Why did you do that?" She wiped her mouth with the back of her hand.

"I'm sorry. I am frazzled after the incident, but I must admit, I enjoyed the kiss."

"Don't ever do that again. Is my mother in there?"

"Your mother is fine. I hate to be the one to tell you, but Max attempted to remarry Becca this morning."

"I don't believe you."

"I'm telling you the truth!"

"That can't be the truth. Where is my mother?"

"Uh, she left through the back door. She said she was going to bed. By the way, she hates Max and wants you to marry me. We'll talk later and make arrangements."

"I don't know what happened in there. But it's over between you and me. I'll go find Mother and get the truth."

Minutes later, Max arrived at the apartment. He called the train station and purchased a ticket to Jacksonville. He gathered his clothes, looked at the jewelry bag, and tossed it in his luggage. Max would give it to his mom one day, maybe for her birthday.

When he checked out of the inn, he paid for his suite and left a message for Becca. **The suite is canceled at 11 a.m. tomorrow. I suggest you make plans to leave Wednesday. You can forget Jake Jones, too. He is marrying Liz.**

Max rode the hotel bus to the train station and called Sydnee and JJ, letting them know he would be home for Christmas after all. He would spend the holidays with friends rather than family.

Liz rushed to her brother's apartment to see Max, but there was no sign of her new boyfriend. She called the front desk clerk and discovered Max had checked out. Liz called Annabelle, who unfortunately did not speak coherently, rambling about an alleged murder plot.

Liz phoned the security office, but everyone had left except the new man on duty for the night. She texted Max to discover why he had left early but got no response. Liz rested in the nearest chair and recalled recent events. *If I heard the situation correctly, Max was about to marry his ex-wife in the chapel. Why would he do that if he wanted to date me? Maybe he realized he loved the lady in red at the family lunch.* Liz understood why; his ex-wife was a beautiful woman.

She tossed and turned most of the night, thinking about the handsome man with the deep voice. Liz decided to return to work after Christmas and visit associations and insurance companies on the east coast closer to home. She must focus on business and forget love.

The Bradford Inn would end the year with an outstanding balance sheet, and she would do even better next year. She would work in her office tomorrow, setting goals and a new schedule. Liz loved her job, and many women chose a career over love. Relationships were too complicated.

Liz recalled the events of the last few days. Max rejected her because she lied, but he said he understood her reason. What happened to his plan of getting to know each other? Something else caused him to choose Becca. *What did Jake do?*

"Never mind, if this is my destiny to live alone, so be it. I'm never going to try to love again. A broken heart hurts too much," Liz whispered.

Max called his dear friend as he stared out the train window.

"Hello."

"Hey, Sydnee, Merry Christmas!"

"Merry Christmas to you, Max. How is Vermont?"

"It has too many people in it."

"Oh? What happened?"

"The story is so crazy; you won't believe it. I will tell it to you in person."

"Alright, we'll have dinner when you return."

"Is the Christmas lunch invitation still open?"

"You are coming home before Christmas?"

"Yeah."

"I'll add a place setting for you. See you at one o'clock on Christmas Day." Sydnee added, "Does Margo need to find a plus one for you?"

"Absolutely not!"

"Wow, I can't wait to hear about your trip."

"Tell the Wildflowers my story may top anything they did in high school."

"Oh, my. Call when you arrive in Madison County."

Max ordered room service. As he observed the scenery out of the window, he wrote his list of why single life was the best choice for males.

"Liz signaled she was a game player with that 'Sarah' story. She lied about her name, job, love for Jake Jones, ownership of The Bradford Inn, and her mother. I wonder what manual she read to learn that skill so well. I played right into her little hands."

Max stared out the window for a while. He was mesmerized by those eyes and that fake, sweet personality. He figured Liz laughed herself to sleep every night. He didn't think any woman could be sneakier than Becca, but Liz Bradford won the Academy Award for best actress.

After his meal, he prepared his bed and turned out the lights. He looked at the passing lights on the streets as the train rolled through towns.

"I will never trust another woman except for the Madison County Wildflowers, Mother, and Marty."

Chapter 20

The morning began at The Bradford Inn on Wednesday with the phone ringing in Liz's apartment. Liz felt sad, lonely, and rejected. She reluctantly answered, "Hello."

"Hey, Beautiful, have you had breakfast yet?"

"Sam, it's early. Why are you awake at this time of day?"

"Meet me at the café. The chef prepared a Christmas pancake that is delicious. Come on. I want to talk to you."

"Thanks, but I will skip the morning meal today."

"Nonsense. Come join me."

Liz agreed to meet her dear friend. In her depression, she failed to eat a decent meal Tuesday. Liz quickly dressed casually, threw makeup on her face to cover her swollen eyes, and grabbed her notebook. She picked up the gift for Sam that she had ordered online.

When Liz arrived at the café, Sam and Annabelle sat with the four adults she remembered from the chapel yesterday. Annabelle saw Liz enter and waved her over. Sam walked toward Liz and hugged her. The two gentlemen rose and offered her a seat.

"Sam, Merry Christmas!" Liz handed a Christmas package to her dear friend.

"Thanks. Please listen to what these guests have to share. Trust me." Sam hugged Liz again.

"Sweetheart, I would like for you to meet Dan and Jill Harvelle of Orlando and Marty and her husband, Charlie Woodson," Annabelle said.

"Hello," Liz spoke softly. Liz looked at her mother. All she wanted to do was get out of the restaurant. *I can't believe Sam was a part of this trick.* She glanced toward Sam as he opened his gift.

Jill noticed Liz's hesitation and said, "Please, we wish to apologize to you for yesterday's events."

"Yes, sweetheart." Annabelle continued, "I don't know exactly what I said to you over the phone last evening, but we must give you accurate information. I asked Sam to call you. Okay?"

Sam put his arm around Liz's chair.

Liz sat and listened as Jill revealed the entire story about Max and Becca and the alleged murder plot, how Becca had manipulated her and Marty into thinking there was a relationship between Max and Becca, and how Max was innocent of everything.

Marty added, "After the chapel fiasco, Max finally explained to everyone who Sarah was."

"What about Sarah?" Liz looked at Sam.

"The notes you left for Max?"

"Yes."

"The clerk assumed a lady was staying at the inn without paying because no woman named Sarah ever registered. He started an investigation that led to the catastrophe in the chapel. Thanks for the gift. I love it."

"Oh, my gosh!" said Liz.

"You see, honey, the whole situation was a comedy of errors," Jill acknowledged.

Everyone continued with breakfast and chimed in as Jill recalled everything with Max since Thanksgiving.

When Jill finished the detailed story, Liz asked, "But why did Max leave the inn and head back to Jacksonville? Why didn't he talk to me?"

Marty commented, "I believe he was so disgusted with Becca and her manipulation of everyone that he decided the situation was too complicated." Marty added, "He looked shocked when he discovered you were one of the owners of the inn and Annabelle's daughter."

Liz reflected on her conversations with Max. She realized that she had never told him about her relationship with Annabelle or the inn because she didn't consider herself an owner. She was an employee. *That was another batch of misinformation.* Liz covered her face and sighed.

Marty added, "Last night, he called me and said he wasn't mad with any of us. When I asked him how he felt about you, he claimed you had chosen Jake. He could tell by how Jake had kissed you when he left the chapel."

Now, Liz understood Jake's kiss! She explained, "Jake is a manipulator. He kissed me outside the chapel and told me Max tried to remarry Becca."

"All of that is a lie," said Jill.

Liz felt obligated to explain her side of the story and how the topic of Annabelle and her ownership of the inn never came up in a conversation.

Dan concluded, "This is one big mess. I'm glad we have everything settled. Nobody will ever believe this situation when we share this Christmas story with our future grandchildren."

"Sam, fire Jake Jones today! I should have listened to you, Liz!"

"Annabelle, he has one more show after tonight, and then he is gone. He has a contract. I suggest I meet with him after his last concert and tell him never to enter the building again."

"You're right!" Annabelle asked, "Sweetheart, what will you do about Max?"

"Max probably doesn't want anything to do with me after everything that happened."

Jill encouraged Liz, "Please don't give up on my son. He needs you."

"What happened to Becca?" asked Liz.

"Dan and I met with that woman last night. We made it clear that she was never to contact our family again. Annabelle has agreed to ban her from The Bradford Inn. And Becca left on the first train out of Wellington today."

"I suggested she seek psychological help," added Dan.

"Mother, is the bellhop still employed with the inn?"

"Yes. You know I have a heart for college students. Chief Lewis and I discussed criminology with the boy late yesterday. I agreed to allow him to follow the chief once a week to see how security works at the inn. He had good intentions, just a little misguided."

"Mr. and Mrs. Harvelle, I thank you for explaining everything. I'm glad I had the opportunity to meet you. I hope the rest of your stay is uneventful." Liz found words difficult. She just wanted to get out of the room before she cried.

"What are you doing today, sweetheart?" asked Annabelle.

"I think I will go with Sam this morning. Discuss the new contracts with him. It was nice meeting you, Marty, and Charlie. Thanks again."

After Liz and Sam left the café, Jill spoke. "Annabelle, I feel responsible for this entire situation. We must put our heads together and give our children another opportunity to meet."

"What do you have in mind?" asked Annabelle.

Dan interrupted, "Jill, you need to stop meddling. Look what just happened here!"

"Honey, we cannot sit back and do nothing. Our kids are miserable!"

Annabelle supported Jill. "I agree. We must get them together. Jill, what are you thinking?"

"Let's see. Christmas Eve is tomorrow." Jill paused.

"You and I will adjust Santa Claus's schedule slightly this Christmas."

Chapter 21

On Christmas Eve, Liz called Sam.

"Hello, Liz"

"I have been thinking."

"Alright."

"I'm going to buy a ticket to Jacksonville."

"What time does the train leave?"

"I'm not going by train."

"That's a long bus ride, sweetheart."

"I'm flying. What do you think of that idea?"

"Well, you remember about that last trip on the plane?"

"Sam, I don't want to think about that!"

"Okay."

"Do you think I'm crazy?"

"No, I think you are in love."

"So, you agree with me about the trip?"

"You will have the opportunity to explain everything without any family interference."

"Yes, that's right. I'll confess about everything."

"And you can practice your speech during the flight."

"Yes, I can do that. Keep my mind busy."

"Just remember."

"Remember what?"

"Don't look out the window."

"Sam!"

"Good luck, sweetheart. I love you, and Max does, too."

On Christmas morning, while Liz sat on the plane, she pulled a sleep mask over her eyes and waited, facing the front. During liftoff, she grabbed the armrests and squeezed tightly.

"Do you need anything?" the flight attendant asked.

"May I have a bottle of water and a bag of peanuts, please?"

"Sure."

"Could I have a blanket, please?" asked Liz when the steward returned as she pulled her sweater closer to her body.

"Yes, here you go."

An hour later, Liz asked the assistant, "Do you have any cheese crackers, please?"

"Yes."

"Do you have half and half tea?"

"Yes, don't you want to remove the sleep mask?"

"No, definitely not!"

After the attendant disappeared again, the little lady sitting next to Liz couldn't wait any longer.

"Dear, I hate to ask, but are you sick? You are shaking!"

"No."

"Do you fly often?"

"No!"

"How about I hold your hand?" The older woman noticed Liz clenching her hands together.

"Okay! That would be nice of you."

"Do you want to take off your gloves?"

"No."

"Would you like to read a book or watch a movie? It's a comedy."

"No, nothing will make me laugh right now."

"Is this your first flight?"

"No. It's an emergency."

"Where are you headed?"

"Hopefully, home."

She focused on Max, his smile, caring, and love as the plane traveled for four hours and fifty-eight minutes. She landed in Jacksonville at 2:00 p.m. and drove a rental car two hours to scenic Cherry Lake in Madison County. Following Mr. Harville's directions, Liz quickly identified Max's rustic house.

The lodge stood on a grassy knoll surrounded by giant, live oak trees with Spanish moss draping over large limbs. A porch went all the way around the residence. Walking hesitantly to the backyard, she found Max fishing off the dock. He didn't see her. She could hear music playing, but it wasn't Jake Jones singing. *He's playing the Doobie Brothers!*

"Sir?"

Max turned around to face Liz.

"Sir, I'm Elizabeth Bradford. Strangers know me as Sarah. Classmates from high school call me Lizzie, but the man who lives in that house and is the best kisser I know calls me Liz."

Max placed his rod and reel on the dock. "Well, hello."

She continued. "I was in the area today, calling on businesses on behalf of The Bradford Inn, of which I own one-third interest. I don't tell people I own one-third interest because I consider myself an employee of the company first."

He slowly walked over to Liz. "This is Christmas. Has any business responded to your professional call today?"

"Not yet, but I'm hoping one business gives me a chance."

"How do you know the man who lives in that house is the best kisser? Do you kiss all your prospects?"

Liz giggled. "No!"

He grinned. Max moved closer and said, "I read in a book that even the best kisser can improve if he practices."

Liz took a step toward Max. "I'm willing to assist this owner in that research."

Max approached Liz, leaned over, and sweetly kissed her. "Merry Christmas, Liz Bradford."

"Merry Christmas, Max Harvelle."

Max kissed Liz again.

"Max, something tells me you knew I was coming here today."

"My mother called and explained; Annabelle called with an apology. Marty texted that you got on an airplane to come to my house. Each said not to tell anyone she called."

"They did? Your dad and I told them not to interfere."

"There's more."

"What?"

"My father called and commanded me to listen to you with open eyes and heart."

"You're kidding!"

"There's more."

"More?"

"Members of our families threatened me. If I did not listen to your apology and explanation, they would move here and live with me forever."

"That's why you were nice to me when I arrived."

"No, Sam called. Is he a black belt in Karate?"

"No."

"I'm glad to know that." Max sighed. "We had an interesting holiday, didn't we?"

"It was different." Liz reflected, "I apologize. I don't understand how I screwed up everything."

"You didn't, by yourself. There was a lot of help from several people."

"Thank you for understanding."

"Do you realize I never asked you for your last name?" asked Max.

"No, when I was around you, I was happy, and all I wanted to do was hold your hand."

"When Marty said you boarded a plane to Jacksonville, I knew you loved me."

"I wasn't afraid."

Max stared at her.

"Well, a little anxious."

Max waited.

"Okay, I was scared. I hope I never have to ride one again to prove I love you."

"You won't."

"Thank you."

"Liz?"

"Yes."

"I'm proud of you. That took guts."

Liz looked pleased.

"You realize our mothers and my sister will not stop meddling until we are married."

"Will they stop then, you think?"

"No," Max laughed.

"I'm sorry about ruining Christmas."

"You didn't. We created our first great memory together. And I had a great Christmas Day. I ate lunch with the Wildflowers of Madison County."

"You never told me how old those ladies are!"

"You don't have to worry about them. If I tried to form a personal relationship with any of those ladies, three men would take turns knocking my teeth out slowly."

"I can't wait to meet them. I brought a present for you." Liz looked into her purse and found a red package with a white bow.

Max unwrapped his gift, the photo of them with Santa Claus, taken at the inn.

"I love it! That was a good day."

"Yes, it was."

"Thanks. You have a present under my Christmas tree."

"I wasn't expecting one, but thank you."

Max grabbed her hand and walked toward the swing near the oak trees. Max looked at the beautiful lake. "If you had not come here, I would have returned to Wellington after Christmas."

"Why?"

"After Mom explained everything from your viewpoint, I knew we had to follow our plan. I'm looking forward to showing you how much I love you."

He leaned to kiss her, but he stopped when he heard voices. Dan, Charlie, Marty, Jill, Annabelle, and a stranger walked toward them.

Dan yelled, "Jill insisted that we catch the next plane after Liz's flight."

"That is not true. Your father insisted we hurry and get here. Didn't he, Annabelle?"

"Yes, you must believe Jill."

Dad said, "Well, we will not allow you two to celebrate your first Christmas without your family."

"Bryan, what are you doing in America?" shouted Liz.

"Who is Bryan?" asked Max, pulling Liz to his side.

"My brother. You stayed in his apartment."

Bryan hugged his sister and whispered, "It's a long story. We'll talk later. Love you."

"I'm glad you are here. Mother, who is running the inn?"

"I left Sam in charge."

Liz introduced her brother, the chef, to Max. Everyone hugged. Laughter and conversation filled the air.

Max said, "I want to welcome everyone to my place. It's great to have my family here for Christmas."

Marty announced, "With all the craziness during the trip, Charlie and I did not find the right time to give you our Christmas present." She looked at Charlie.

Charlie added, "Mom, Dad, you will be grandparents in June."

Jill shouted and started crying; Dan grabbed Marty and shook Charlie's hands. Max hugged his sister.

Annabelle exclaimed, "Liz, did you hear that? Jill is becoming a grandmother."

"Yes, I heard the announcement, Mother." Liz hugged Marty. "I am so happy for you, Marty."

"To prepare for being a future grandmother, hopefully myself, I would love to go shopping with you, Jill."

Dan asked, "Do we know if it's a boy or girl?"

Charlie responded, "It's a girl."

The women said "Ahh" in unison.

Max grabbed his sister. "This is wonderful news. I can't wait. Maxine is a great name."

"We're still working on names, but I won't remember that one."

Jill cackled with excitement. "There are so many cute outfits for little girls. Let's decorate her room with pinks and purples. What do you think about that, Annabelle?"

"I know a vendor who makes gorgeous baby quilts. She can use those colors in her design. Have you seen the little black dress with ruffles for baby girls? I love it."

"And they design shoes, purses, and hats for every outfit?" Jill grabbed Marty and Annabelle and started planning. Dan and Charlie talked to each other as they followed the ladies inside.

Annabelle's cell phone rang. She asked the caller, "What do you mean I owe you $100? What bet?"

Max asked, "Your mother is a gambler?"

"No." Liz asked, "Mother, who did you make a bet with?"

Annabelle answered, "It's nothing. It's a private matter, sweetheart." Annabelle moved away. "Okay, I'll pay you the one hundred bucks, but I think you had inside information!" Annabelle paused. “I will write you a check when I return. Of course, it’s good.”

Liz whispered, “It sounds like she made a bet with Sam. Max, please don’t make a wager with him. He knows everything.”

“Thanks for the tip.”

Dan yelled, “Son, we’re going inside to watch football. Come on, Bryan. What is your favorite college team?”

“I’m an FSU fan,” as Bryan followed the men into the house.

“So are we.”

The family members stepped onto the porch and went inside Max’s home. Max grabbed Liz’s hand and pulled her back.

“We may be off the hook,” whispered Max.

“Yes, but only for six months.”

“Hey, I know the best way to celebrate this day.”

“What are you thinking?” asked Liz.

Chapter 22

"It's five o'clock and time for my daily cruise around Cherry Lake. Hurry before the family remembers us."

Max grabbed Liz's hands and pulled her to the party barge. Once on board, he opened a bottle of champagne and handed her a flute.

"Here's to getting to know each other, finding lasting love," he added after a pause, "and avoiding parental interference."

"Amen."

Liz's phone rang. Immediately after that, Max's phone rang. Both answered their phones at the same time. Liz listened to Annabelle, and Max heard Jill's instructions.

Annabelle began, "Sweetheart, do you think you will have a spring or Christmas wedding? It can't be in June because the baby is due that month. We could stop in New York and shop for wedding dresses and stuff on the flight home. We also need to think about your bridesmaids and their dresses. We are assuming you want a big reception. Don't worry. Jill and I will handle the difficult tasks. However, we will hire a wedding planner. Jill knows a good one from Orlando. Also, everything depends on where you have the wedding. There is so much to do. What are you thinking? Liz? Are you there?"

"Max, I know you just got home, but planning a wedding takes time. Annabelle wants to meet the wedding planner from Orlando that I like. We will drive down there while she is in town and meet with the planner, or we will do a Zoom call if you and Liz want to participate. Have you decided on the venue? Between you and me, I hope you choose Orlando. All our friends are there. Son, you are not responding. Are you there?"

Both Max and Liz laid their phones on the console of the barge. Standing by Max as he guided the boat to the center of the lake, Liz looked at the beauty of the water framed by old cypress trees and tall pines. He pushed a button, and the Doobie Brothers softly sang "Black Water."

Liz glanced at Max with surprise and a smile. He was playing her kind of music. No more Jake Jones!

"Did you purchase rock and roll CDs for me?"

"I didn't purchase them; they are on loan from the Wildflowers."

Max placed his hands around her shoulders and pulled her to him. Liz closed her eyes, thankful for forgiveness and second chances. They swayed to rock and roll music. Neither Liz nor Max would forget the Christmas they met on a train. She thought about writing a book about it but decided against it. Who would believe it anyway?

"Liz?" asked Annabelle.

"Son? Dan said to tell you FSU won the game. Annabelle and I have fabulous ideas to make your wedding day memorable!"

Max and Liz watched the sunset as they thought about their future together.

"Liz?" asked Max.

"Yes."

"Let's take a selfie."

"Okay."

Max immediately sent the photo to someone.

"Where did you send our second photo?"

"I emailed it to the Wildflowers of Madison County."

"Why?"

"Sydnee, Margo, and Diane will arrive in about thirty minutes. They won't wait until tomorrow to say hello to the woman in that photo. You are going to love the Wildflowers and Madison County. Merry Christmas, Liz."

The End

Dear Reader,

Thanks for purchasing this novel. I hope you enjoyed reading this second book in the Madison County series as much as I did writing it. I created this book to share a story about Christmas that made people laugh. Christmas is a beautiful holiday, but it is also a sad time. We remember friends and family who are no longer with us. Many have relatives serving in the military who are overseas. Some people are sick in the hospital, and others have parents or grandparents living in nursing homes.

Over the last two years, many homes have had empty seats at the dining table due to Covid-19. My novel cannot replace those special people in our lives, but it can give those relatives struggling with the loss of loved ones a few minutes of laughter during a time of tears.

In 1968, I married three days after Christmas. Before our first Christmas as a married couple, my husband came to discuss gifts. I remember this conversation like yesterday, but it occurred over fifty years ago.

Bobby asked, "What would you like for Christmas?"

I said, "I don't need anything. Give me what you want to give me."

And Bobby waited silently. Finally, I realized he wanted me to ask him the same question. So, I did.

He pulled a folded piece of paper with twenty-five items listed on it out of his right pocket. Each item had a number, the name of the store where I could purchase the gift, the aisle number and which shelf the thing was on, and if the rack was on the left or right side of the aisle. I looked at my cute husband, who was excited about his personal gift list. I told him I knew everything on his list except number seventeen. I had no clue what that was.

Bobby responded, "Don't worry. Go to the old hardware store in Madison and tell the owner, Mr. Phillips, you are my wife and there to get my gift. He will go upstairs and get it. He is saving it for me."

Bobby received everything on his list. He had been good all year. Through the years, his list got shorter but more expensive. This ritual happened every year until 1989. That year, he requested a huge, durable pot for cooking food (like chili) for large gatherings.

He told me I could find that specific pot at the local Farmers' Cooperative Store.

For the first time, I requested a gift. I asked Bobby to purchase a Mont Blanc pen for me. That's all I wanted. I checked under the tree frequently but never saw a small box shaped like a Mont Blanc pen.

After we had opened our gifts on Christmas morning, Bobby asked, "Where is my pot? Was it too big to wrap?" (This was the first year he did not get everything on his list!)

I responded, "I guess it's in the same place as my Mont Blanc pen!"

On December 28th, our anniversary, I received my Mont Blanc pen, and my husband received his chili pot. We continued this gift tradition every year of our marriage.

Christmas is more difficult now because my husband passed in 2018. However, I remember 1969 and 1989 every Christmas morning, and I laugh. If you don't have a funny Christmas story to remember, I hope you will enjoy reading my book and re-reading it every Christmas.

Whose story is next in Book Three in the Madison County series? Grace discovers her history, JJ marries the love of his life, and a stranger finds hope by meeting the Wildflowers.

I hope you will write an honest review of this novel on Amazon. Please join my email list to get discounts and early-release opportunities for future books.

Mary

P.S. Now, I know what you're thinking. What was the name of gift number seventeen on Bobby's list? It was a whittling rock. I apologize to my male friends for not knowing what it was. Bobby never let me forget it, either.

About the Author

Mary Buchanan writes women's fiction with a touch of humor and a lot of heart. She is a retired educator who graduated from Florida State University and Nova Southeastern University with degrees in educational leadership and speech communication.

Mary spent her career encouraging and inspiring students and her fellow teachers alike. These days, when she isn't brushing up on her photography hobby, she loves traveling with friends and enjoying the beauty of wildflowers.

Visit Mary at
Website: MaryBuchananAuthor.com
Facebook/com/MaryBuchanan/Author

Made in the USA
Columbia, SC
15 March 2024